CORN MAZE

OLESIA PARKER

This work is a fictional novel. Names, characters, places, and incidents are the product of Olesia Parker's imagination. Any resemblance to actual events, locales, or persons, living or dead, is coincidental.

Corn Maze

Copyright © 2022 Olesia Parker

All rights reserved. No part of this book may be reproduced or used in any matter without the prior written permission of the copyright owner, except for the use of brief quotations in a book review.

Paperback: 978-1-7375847-5-9

First paperback edition December 2022

PROLOGUE

I'd like to think I haven't always been like *this,* but truth be told, I can't remember. Some days are better than others, while most just seem like some distant distraction not even I can follow. I'm sure it will get better; I can only hope it will.

I crave connection, I crave relationships and being free. Now? I just wanna be normal. It seems so simple, but it's my brain that overly complicates everythin' to a 'T'. My story isn't all that different from that of anyone else, except the parts that could be turned into a horror/thriller franchise.

I never really liked horror films or thrillers; I don't like to be kept on edge, never knowin' what's gonna happen next. I look online and read the synopsis of every movie before I watch it. I read the last page of every book before beginnin' the first chapter. My two best friends, Colton and Abilene, love them though, and I don't have the heart to tell them no every Friday night.

I live in a small town in Louisianna. There's not much to do besides gossip and ride the canal if you haven't already. Everyone already knows everyone, even before you're born. If I dared say one word, the entire town would hear about it within minutes.

I like distractions, but I assume there's no use in delayin' the inevitable any longer than I should. I never know where to start because my memories have pooled themselves into one pond, leavin' any remainin' rivers, dry. Mama says I should stop daydreamin'.

"Impure, tarnished, used".

Empty,

My name is Millie Maye, welcome to my hell.

CHAPTER I

I was a kid, just a stupid little kid. I didn't know any better, and maybe neither did he. I sometimes think I made it up, that it never really happened. Even my ghost ain't able to recognize between fact and fiction.

"Hunter, why don't ya go outside and show Millie the koi pond?" his mama smiled.

I sat on mama's lap, pickin' at my ear like mites got in. She grabbed onto my hands and told me to stop scratchin' or else the infection would get worse. She wasn't wrong, I was a pest in my ear's recovery, but it was too itchy not to pick.

She placed me on the ground, encouragin' me to follow her friend's son out the door. His crooked smirk widened as he scratched his freshly buzzed head of brown hair. He was taller than me by a whole foot, most people were.

I looked back at mama; she tucked a strand of her short and dark brown hair behind her ear and I smiled when it fell out once more.

"But I don't wanna" I reached. "I'll stay with you".

"Go outside and play" mama said, showin' her pearlies. "Faith and I are fixin' to go dig up a few blueberry bushes".

"I wanna go with you".

"Darlene and I'll be back before ya know it, peanut" Faith said. *"If ya need anythin', ask Zach, he's upstairs with his PlayStation".*

I watched as mama and her tall friend left the kitchen and out the front door, leavin' Hunter and I alone. My heart sped and my mind shut down. I told myself mama was comin' back fer me soon, that she wasn't gonna leave how daddy left when I was seven.

I counted in my head and Hunter laughed, he knew I was nervous, anxious, even scared.

"Yer such a child" he nudged and walked past me, stoppin' at the bottom of the stairs to yell up at his older brother. *"Zach, Millie and I are goin' fer a walk".*

"I don't care".

Hunter towered over me before walkin' to the front door. He stopped to look at me with his squinted brown eyes and I couldn't help but think of how many times he must've fallen from the ugly tree, hittin' every branch on the way down.

"We're goin'".

I dunno why I listened.

I quickened my steps and followed him, hearin' the door shut with a hard bang as we ventured outside and into the cool breeze of summer. The sun was shinin' warm on my skin, and the tree's static sounds calmed my mind.

Hunter showed me the chickens, the new koi pond they built, and the horses. They had a whole field of rabbits, but they were hard to see cause it was their entire woods that fenced them in. He told me we could go and find 'em, and I stupidly liked the idea.

I followed behind him on the sandy path into the woods of pine and evergreens. I didn't pay no attention to the trees that looked the same, our path that disappeared, the rabbits I never saw. I didn't pay no attention and it was all my fault.

I couldn't even be mad it happened, cause I ain't done nothin' to stop it.

Our feet walked in circles I thought I'd seen before, and he asked if I knew my way. I told him "No" and he smirked, even smiled. Further and further, we ventured into the unforgivin' forest that'd soon change my life.

I didn't even pay no attention to the pine in the air, the crunch of fallen sticks under my feet. I didn't do much besides blindly follow him with sweaty palms and a curious look while my heart sat at the bottom of my stomach laughin' at me.

What a fool.

We stopped at the edge of the woods, overlookin' a lush cornfield the sun lit like it was the heavens. I didn't know it was hell. I rubbed my sweaty palms against my jeans and looked at Hunter. He stared at me like I was the last thing he wanted to see.

Disgusted.

I turned back around to look at the corn field and I wish I hadn't. I shouldn't have. Jesus save me because I couldn't.

I froze when the sound of metal clanked against metal and my thoughts formed the picture of his belt loosenin'. I froze when his pants dropped and he came closer. I froze when he jumped on me and I froze, and I froze, and I froze.

I drowned and was blinded from the pictures and sounds and the new memories my body was facin' that I'd never remember. There was nothin', and I was nothin'. I didn't even know if it hurt or not, cause I wasn't alive.

There was no God, no savior to pull me up and out from the darkness. There was no feelin' of me inside my body because it did not exist. I was dead, a million times, I was dead.

And then I snapped, adorned by God too late.

"I have an infection" I screamed. "I'm infected and I'm not supposed- I have- I have" I could hardly speak through my screams.

By the grace of God, Hunter got off me and I stared at the ground as he walked away. I stared at the pine needles dug into my hands, the sap I knew stained my knees. I didn't have time to cry, to pity myself, or pull my pants back up, cause Hunter was movin' too fast without me.

"Wait!" I called to him like the idiot I was. "Wait, please, I dunno how to get back".

He stopped and let me catch up to him, my entire body was sore, tired from- I was starin' at the cornfields and my body was tired- I was tired from our walk.

I didn't say a word, neither did he. He took turns I didn't remember, walked fast then slow to see if I'd be his copycat. My mouth dried through my parted lips and I sucked in a sharp breath of air. I looked at my palms and picked away at the dried sap stuck to 'em.

When I looked up, I was lost. Not only in my mind, but my thoughts too that silenced themselves quickly and reprimanded me fer not showin' interest in the uncharted map that lied ahead.

"H-Hunter?" I barely breathed. "Hunter where are you? This isn't funny" tears began to cloud my vision. "Hunter?".

I ran 'round shrubs, pierced the bottoms of my feet on pinecones and acorns. He was nowhere to be found. He was nowhere to be found and I hated myself fer hatin' his absence. I needed him, and he knew it. He knew it. He knew it. A thousand times, he knew it.

My lungs got weak and I begged once more fer him. I gave him my power and let him keep it fer decades after. I looked like a chicken runnin' around without its head before supper.

"Ya think yer too big fer yer britches? If I had my druthers, I wouldn't bring ya back" he spat. "Count yerself lucky".

Why was I relieved? Why did I smile when he came back? What was I but a foolish varmint to him and myself? I was deranged, it was my fault. I was cynical, it was my fault.

Mama yelled at me when I got back, told me she had somewhere else to be and I wasted her time. It was my fault, I shouldn't have been so stupid. I shouldn't have been so willin' to go off into the woods with a stranger I knew fer years like you would a friend.

It was my fault.

CHAPTER II

"Millie?" Abilene shook my arm. "Aren't ya excited?".

The curly orange haired girl smiled at me with her crooked teeth and I mimicked her enthusiasm. I would've been lyin' if I said I wasn't. Mama never let me into the school system, I dunno why, but I think Abilene had somethin' to do with convincin' her to put me in.

Mama called the school weeks ago and told em' Abes and I were to have the same schedule, and there was no arguin' with Darlene. My mama was the toughest lady this town ever did know, and she wasn't gonna' let some school board director ruin my first and last year.

"Yeah" I whispered, followin' her into the crowded halls of our small school.

I felt like a hacky sack, pushed from one person to another. I thought new kids were supposed to stand out louder than the bell switchin' classes. I didn't mind it though, I wanted to stay hidden, covered under the sheet of loud laughs and smilin' faces.

"We're almost there" Abilene pulled me into a small classroom, packed at the very end of the hall. "I don't like doin' a whole lot in the morn', so art it is".

We sat at the back of the room, feet danglin' from the high chairs to the unnecessarily tall tables. The room looked like my home, decorated in items only a hoarder would find useful. Near the front of the room, there were five walls connected to the floor and ceilin', you could push and pull 'em apart if you needed somethin'.

The short and plump teacher walked in late with a coffee in hand. She wore a frown that told me any question I had would be barkin' up the wrong tree. She dimmed the lights and quickly put our syllabus on the board, ignorin' introductions, classroom safety, and required materials.

"Mrs. Sprange is always like this" Abilene quietly laughed. "She's already got her favorites, best keep ya head down and keep busy".

We began our first project, which was really just a waste of time. It was nothin' more than a sketch of ourselves so Sprange could see where we were at. I thought my drawin' was trash, but then I saw Abes. We snickered amongst ourselves and Sprange gave us a dartin' glare.

"Keep ya head down", right.

Mama never let me do art, told me it was a waste of time, that I had better things to do. She wanted me to do somethin' useful, like bein' a doctor or lawyer. I think she knew I wouldn't admit to nothin' though, no one in this town ever did.

The loud sound of class's end chimed over the room's speakers and the class quickly dispersed throughout the halls. I followed Abe to physics and then environmental science; both were just as borin'. Though mama "homeschooled" me, it was really just me doin' it all. Darlene worked too much to teach me anythin'.

It wasn't all that bad. If I finished my work then I could do whatever I wanted. I didn't have bells, teachers, or syllabuses tellin' me what I could and couldn't do.

"Earth to Mil" Abilene waved her hand in front of my face.

My vision cleared and I looked 'round, I was standin' in the cafeteria line. I gave Abilene a smile as she guided me through, tellin' me what was trash and what wasn't. She even showed me how to pay, though mama's income expelled me from it.

The cafeteria wasn't anythin' grand, same as the school. I didn't have any expectations goin' in anyway since my town was as poor as field mice. I think that's partially why daddy left, said mama didn't have a pot to pee in let alone a window to throw it out of.

"Long time no see, Millie bean" said the body that sat to my right, smushin' me between Abilene and him.

Colton. I tried to be poetic describin' him to mama when I was younger, but she didn't like that. Told me all men were good-fer-nothin' cheat bags. Considerin' all things, I got her point. But I think she was just usin' daddy leavin' us an excuse to keep me to herself.

Still, I dunno why she got so mad at me that day. All I said was he had sandy brown hair like a bird, amber eyes like abita river, tan skin like he'd been workin' on his daddy's farm, and full lips that I wanted to kiss- I rest my case.

Technically a year above me and Abilene, Colton stayed behind since he was studyin' classes at the police academy our rival school offered. He was goin' places, that's what he always said. Told me he was goin' to get me outta this town.

"How are you liking this place?" he shoved a piece of bread into his mouth.

"It's- uh- not that bad" I looked away, blush creepin' up.

"You haven't changed a bit" he smirked, this time throwin' a chip into his mouth.

"You haven't changed a bit" a group of loud boys paraded our corner.

The sunlight pierced his warm eyes into pools of honey as he rolled them far behind his head. He mouthed 'sorry' and Abilene nudged me with her elbow.

"Trevor, Austin, and Brooks" he leaned in to whisper. "Stay strong".

He said somethin' like he told 'em about me and to take what they said with some salt. To be honest, I didn't pay no attention to a single word he said, I was lost in his eyes and swimmin' in his scent.

"Someone's got it hard" Abe sat up straight with a whisper.

I shot her a darin' glare and didn't care lookin' back at Colton, I was too embarrassed. I mean, it's not like I'd try anythin' with him, I was too scared. Too much trauma is what I called it from them self-healing books I seen.

"Don't pay her any attention" Colton touched my elbow and my eyes questioned. "Give it a hot sec".

"Hey, Brooks" Abilene snorted at the blue eyed and blond hair man while tuckin' a lock of hair behind her pale ears.

If I didn't understand now, I was too dumb fer everythin'. The way she looked at that boy was how I looked at my KFC bowl. Starved fer more, especially since the portions were so small.

"This must be the famous Millie y'all talk about" one of the boys, Austin, said. "Pleasure to meet your acquaintance".

He took my hand before I knew it and tried leavin' a kiss on my skin. I didn't like bein' touched, never had and never will, and nothin' was ever gonna change that. Though my thoughts were clear as rain, my body couldn't move, somethin' about fear I guess.

Luckily fer me, Colton smacked that boys hand right outta his face and it fell where it belonged, at his side.

"I ain't do nothin' wrong" he rubbed his hand and sat across from us.

I spent the rest of lunch listenin' to Colton talk about the police academy he was takin' at the other school, still didn't understand why he had to stay back a year. Abilene cut in here and there to make jokes how he'd leave us all to become some high and mighty guy. He assured me he wouldn't.

Bell broke off again and Colton and his friends left Abilene and I to walk alone to next period, and then the next, and the next. School was painfully borin', I didn't see myself makin' no friends, except for the two I already had. I knew other kids were gonna be callin' me 'weird', 'loner', and 'stuck up'.

By the time school was out, I could hardly stand. I ain't never been in no prison, but that's sure what high school felt like. It woulda been an understatement to say I was glad to get outta there. Back in the halls, I bumped into blind bodies one after the other, and Abe compared me to a hockey puck.

"I'm just gonna go g-" Abilene's voice disappeared in the midst of chaotic bodies.

I walked to my locker and messed 'round with the lock before givin' up and fishin' fer the sticky note in my back pocket. *22-13-40*, and it opened. Grabbed my bag and teacup; which was really just a fancy way of saying mason jar, and headed fer the parkin' lot.

Only, I couldn't find it. I liked to think I was a smart girl, but even the simple layout of the school had already gotten the best of me. I sighed deeply and kept my head down as I followed the busy bodies to where I could only assume was outside.

People knocked into me left and right, like I was some kinda toy to 'em. I pulled my elbows in closer to me, but someone else had different ideas. They pulled me into a small hall with a dead end and I fell to me knees.

"Watch where you're goin" I dusted off my jeans and stood.

Somethin' didn't feel right, somethin' in me told me to run. I looked up and my stomach dropped, sweat already begun to bead my forehead before I realized why it wasn't the temperature.

It was him, only he was different. His hair wasn't buzzed short, it grew to his shoulders in brown waves. And he wasn't just a few inches taller than me no more, he surpassed that. He put a pale arm on my shoulder and grabbed tightly onto my bones.

"Count yerself lucky".

"How's yer mama 'n them?" he asked with a smile

I looked back and forth between his face and arm, not sure of what to do. I wanted him off me, that was fer sure. There ain't nothin' in the world that coulda convinced me otherwise. I backed away and his arm fell back to his side.

"Cat got yer tongue?" his disgustin' smile diminished. "I didn't know yer mama was lettin' you join society. Let me take you home".

"No" I whispered.

"C'mon" he moved a strand of hair behind my ear. "I have thirty minutes".

As fast as he moved in, he backed away. Her shoes clacked too close to us fer him to do whatever it was I was gonna let him do, unwillingly. Abilene popped her head 'round the corner, and with her usual dramatics, grabbed her heart and told me she'd been lookin' fer me everywhere.

"I was just gonna take her home" Hunter propped up. "Her mama and mine are really close friends, I know where she lives".

"So do I" Abilene smirked.

"Ready?" I pushed pass Hunter and stood behind Abilene's towerin' height.

"Actually, can ya take me back too?" she batted her ocean eyes.

"What about your truck?" panic cursed my lips.

"It's not workin'. I thought ya were already there when I checked, so I started it, well, tried to. Lord willin' and the creek don't rise, daddy's gonna give me an earful when I get home".

"Of course" he made way fer the exit. "After y'all, ladies".

I tried tellin' Abilene I didn't want to go with him, that I'd rather walk by myself and get bit by an opossum than sit in his truck, but he was in range. Ever since that day, I started rememberin' my surroundings.

So there I was, learnin' how many tiles it took to reach the outside, and how many parkin' spots until we came to his beat up blue chevy truck. He opened the passenger door for Abilene and me, and I cautiously watched him look 'round for peepin' eyes.

"You should get in first" he told me, squattin' into his spot.

There were only three seats; his, a small middle, and the far passenger side. Abilene was quick to shove me in, not pickin' up any of the bad juju vibes I was sendin' her way. She gave him the directions to her house and he was quick to be on his way, tellin' us he didn't have much time.

I didn't say a word as I sat between them. My heart was beatin' and my body was stiffer than a metal pole in the dead of winter. It sounded like Abe was flirtin' with him, then again, she had no reason not to. I never told her or anyone what he did to me. Truth be told, I had a hard time rememberin' it too.

When his tires hit the dirt roads, I leaned onto Abe so I didn't accidentally touch him. Sometimes I even wondered if he remembered what he did to me. I saw him a few times after that day, but I always avoided him, didn't even say hello.

Mama said I was actin' rude.

Sometimes I even wondered if I dreamt the whole thing and nothin' ever happened, but my body knew, my heart too. They shouldn't go so painfully numb when his name comes 'round.

"Earth to Millie" Abilene waved her hand in front of my face. "I'll see ya tomorrow. Pick ya up 'round, oh wait. I'll call yer line and let ya know tonight what's up".

She slammed the door and I quickly jumped into the passenger seat, puttin' my bag in the middle as a useless barrier. I watched as she crossed the fresh green lawn and opened the door to her spacious home. Her and her family were well off in this town, not in others, but they had a lot of lead-way in ours cause of it.

Hunter waited fer her to get inside before drivin' off towards my place, only, he was takin' the wrong turns. I played with my nails, chewed on the sides of my mouth, did anythin' to distract myself from the fears boilin' in my stomach.

> *Our feet walked in circles I thought I seen before, and he asked if I knew my way. I told him no and he smirked, even smiled. Further and further, we ventured into the unforgivin' forest that changed my life.*
>
> *I walked and walked fer minutes that seemed like bloody hours compared to the stupidity that lied awake in my body. It was my fault, all of it. I could've said no,*

I could've run to mama and begged her more to let me stay with her.

If only I had tried harder.

"Ya really do space out" he unbuckled himself.

What? Did I close my eyes? His truck was parked alongside the road, not a single creation in sight, except for the fields of soy to the left and corn on the right.

He said nothin', just stared at me like I was some hopless puppy-dog he found on the side of the road. He placed a hand on my bag and moved it to the floor, scootchin' in to take its place.

"Yer a hard girl to find, ya know that?" his breath stank like chew, fillin' up his truck. "Don't wanna talk? That's fine, there's other things we can do that don't involve talkin".

"Take me back" I whispered.

"Millie" his fingers caressed my cheek and I pushed him away.

God, I relived everythin' all over again. The sounds, the scents. The feelin' of wind on my body when he finished, the pricklin' needles of pines that couldn't protect me like they do durin' them storms.

"Take me back, take me back, take me back!" I screamed.

"Fine, fine" he raised his arms. "Don't get yer panties in a twist".

I never looked at him, didn't care to see what his face looked like. I thought it might've been worse if I did. I do that a lot, avoid eye contact. Mama said the eyes are the window to the soul. If I can't see theirs, then they sure as hell can't see mine.

He drove fast to my house, cussin' under his breath like I did somethin' wrong. It wasn't my fault, but it was, cause I was the idiot who got into the truck. Even though nothin' happened, still, somethin' happened.

He turned onto my road, filled with dirt and potholes like the moon's craters. My body relaxed and seized at the same time. I didn't know whether to be relieved or scared straight.

Mama and I had decent land, thirty acres, our trailer sittin' dead in the middle of it. Still, there wasn't enough of it fer me to run away.

Get me out.

I didn't even give him a chance to start up the driveway before I jumped out. I said nothin', counted to ten, and ripped open his side door. My feet hit the ground, knockin' me off of em', but I got up fast.

"Jesus, Millie" he braked the truck. "You coulda-".

"Thanks fer the ride" I ran up the dirt driveway without a single glance back.

"Yer a real tease" he yelled at me before rippin' outta the driveway. "And I'm gonna get ya for it".

As soon as I heard him turn off the road and onto the other, I stopped. My hands propped on my knees, and I knew mama would give me an earful later fer gettin' stains on my jeans. I drowned in my thoughts, wishin' I would just die instead of wonderin' if he was gonna come back or not.

I took one deep breath before the melodies of the birds brought me back and the breeze through the evergreen forest perked up my spine. *Everythins' okay*, they told me, whoever *they* were.

The trailer finally came in sight and I hadn't been more excited in my life than I was fer the chippin' green paint and tin roof of our home. I dashed up the four stairs of our makeshift porch and I walked inside.

There ain't much to it. You walked into the dinin'/livin' room, kitchen to the left, two bedrooms to the right, and a bathroom in between. Opposite of the front door, was the back, but I guess that just depend on how you saw it.

I set my bag down and didn't care enough to look at the overload of useless work I had to do by tomorrow's day. My body was tired, drained of everythin' but the ability to eat. I walked into the kitchen and kept the lights off, helpin' mama with the bills like that was the only thing I could do fer her.

She left me a note on our white and textured fridge and I raised it to the window fer better readin'.

"Workin' double shift, see you tomorrow. XOXO-mama".

It's not like mama and I didn't get along, we did, really well. Today was probably one of the first days I was glad to be home alone since daddy left. The only secret I ever held from her was Hunter, one I wouldn't mind dyin' with.

I took my head off the fridge and stopped leanin' on it too. I grabbed my dinner from the freezer, opened the box, stabbed some holes through the plastic, and threw it into the microwave fer five minutes.

I folded up mama's note and walked it to my room, placin' it in a small wooden box all her notes went into. I didn't have the heart to throw 'em away.

My tired legs carried me into the small bathroom, where we had a sink, toilet, and a snug stand-up shower. I was kinda happy we couldn't afford a lot of food, there was no way a plump Millie could fit into it the shower.

I turned on the sink, let it run fer a few seconds for the yellow to leave, and I began washin' my face. My mind was racin' like a million horses 'round a single track, and each horse had somethin' wrong with it.

Mama didn't have a lot of friends, the only one she really did have was Faith. I wasn't gonna be the reason why she didn't have her either. The only reason why she had me was cause daddy didn't want me. He took me when he left mama the first time, but gave me back, sayin' I looked too much like her.

I wiped my hand on the mirror, examinin' my face to make sure he was right. There was just one thing wrong with what daddy said, I didn't look a whole lot like mama. My eyes were hazel green like his and I even had the same tan skin.

The only difference was my hair and height. I got mama's long brown hair, though hers was cut short. I was even a few inches less than mama, puttin' me right at five and a half feet tall. Daddy was almost six feet and his hair was light brown, even blond in color.

I wiped off my face and leaned on the sink with both hands. I looked more like daddy than I did mama, and I think that made her sad too. I was a totem of failure that constantly reminded them of each other's failed promises.

"He just didn't want you, Millie" I whispered to no one but myself.

He didn't want you.

CHAPTER III

It'd been a few months since I started my last year in school, and I still hadn't adjusted properly. Everyday seemed like the one before and the next that was to come. I went to all my mornin' classes, ate lunch with Abilene, Colton, and his friends. I still hadn't made any new ones, but that was whatever.

I was top student in all my classes. Turns out, school really did suck. Education, however, did not. I learned more things in one week of self studyin' than I did in a few months of public school. Maybe it was just my town, but there weren't any sharp tools in the toolbox there.

I started beatin' myself up fer not joinin' the extension program Colton did. He always seemed so happy comin' back from the next town over, seemed like he was gonna be doin' better things with his life. I didn't mind, just thinkin' about his success and happiness put a smile on my face.

Wished I coulda hung out with him more, though he was smilin', he was always busy. Workin' a job after school, then another after the first. I dunno when he ever got anythin' done, always on his toes like he was. The only thing that bothered me was I couldn't spend enough time with him like how I wanted.

Abe, Colton, and I always played together when we were younger. Times were different now, we grew up and started havin' feelins' we weren't supposed to have I guess. So I just had to be okay with seein' him fer the twenty minutes of lunch we got.

I made sure to avoid Hunter when I could, but he started showin' up earlier fer his volunteerin' with the football team. I thought once the colder months came it meant he'd leave me alone, but I guess there were indoor versions of the things he had to do.

"Let me drive ya home" his voice crept from behind, just as his hand on my shoulder.

I kept walkin' straight, avoidin' the dirty glares of jealous girls I didn't care existed. I didn't care if they wanted the man clingin' to my back, cause I wanted him gone. I pushed him off me and walked even faster down the hall.

His laugh was loud as he called back to me, tellin' me he'd catch up with me sooner than later. I hoped that woulda been the last time I saw him, but God had other plans fer me it seemed.

He tried walkin' home with me one time when I physically refused a ride. He even tried to stuff me into his truck, which he continuously parked near the woods.

I didn't scream, I did nothin', and he didn't stop. I even had my feet on the edge of the seat while he pushed my shoulders in.

Colton was there, I think he saved me that day. He was doin' a few laps 'round the school fer his police trainin' when he saw us. As soon as Hunter saw him, he let me go. Colton asked what happened, but I kept my head down and said nothin'.

I was even a real sting on the cheek when I left him with Hunter and didn't thank him. I was too embarrassed, too weak. I felt myself goin' numb, which usually meant I was about to disassociate with myself again.

Colton asked once after that day what happened, but I told him to mind his P's and Q's cause we were at the movies. Ever since then, he never brought it up. I think he believed whatever lie Hunter came up with. It was all cattywampus if you ask me.

After every last class, I ran from my locker to Abilene's car, and when she couldn't drive me home, I walked. It wasn't too bad, only a short four mile walk back home. I took the back roads too, so no one could see me and make up some rumor I knew I'd care too much about.

So there I was, walkin' down the road. The sun shinin' on my face, wearin' the same torn up gym shoes, makin' my way home. I knew mama was workin' a double, so I didn't bother comin' up with some lie in my head about why I was walkin'.

She saw me comin' home on my feet one day and yelled at me fer not askin' Hunter fer a ride. Apparently, she talked with Faith and I had made Hunter upset with the unladylike way I was actin'.

"Millie" she looked across my face. "Faith told me Hunter's been volunteerin' at yer school fer football. Why don't you let a nice young man like that drive you home, hmm?".

"I'm fine walkin', mama" I slopped onto the couch.

"Jesus help us all. I better not catch you doin' this again. You never know who can drive right up and

snatch ya" she sat next to me, puttin' an arm 'round. "I'm worried fer you, Mills".

"Huh?" I stupidly asked.

I knew she was just worried fer me. That's exactly what daddy did when he took me, and it was the last time I saw him.

I was just sittin' at home alone, watchin' my cartoons when he followed me to the house, knocked down the door and stuffed my clothes into a trash bag.

Had me fer only a month before givin' me back. It was a whole thing, the police got involved and I had to be interviewed by a bunch of people. I tried tellin' them daddy didn't hurt me, but mama thinks otherwise.

"I just want ya to have a good life, with a good man. Maybe even settle down, have some kids, and raise 'em to be good people".

"And you think I wanna do that with Hunter?" I got up in disgust. "He's not the only fish in the sea, and besides, he's uglier than sin on Sunday".

"What's wrong with that boy?" she voiced an angry tone. "He's a fine young man, volunteers fer his community, he's even gettin' a job with the police".

"I don't like him, mama!" I yelled. "He's slower than molasses and he's as useless as tits on a bull!".

"Well, I'll be" she smiled. "There's someone else you've taken a fancy to, isn't there?".

My skin blushed and painted my face pinker than a pig in the sun. I argued with her, sayin' there was no *one, even though she was right. I fancied Colton, and if I told her, the whole town would know it, includin' him.*

I was never gonna do anythin', neither was he, so we'd sit by ourselves and not say a thing. I told mama not to worry, that I was sorry, and she apologized fer gettin' so worked up. I knew where she was comin' from, a failed marriage would get you kicked to the back pew of church.

"I don't want you to end up like me, that's all I'm sayin'. Okay?" she gave me a hug, squeezin' my arms.

I let my hands trace the tall grass, tree trunks, and waist high shrubs that grew alongside the road as I walked home. It was kinda fun, sometimes I'd close my eyes and guess what kind of plants I was touchin', made connectin' to my gatherin' ancestors more fun.

A pebble got stuck in my sneakers so I pulled off the road and leaned on a tree while I worked off my shoe. Only, I shook it out and watched the smallest piece of gravel fall from the inside. I balanced on one leg, fittin' it back on.

Just as I stepped back onto the road, the sound of slow tires made me quicken myself. I didn't know who it was, or what they were lookin' fer, but they weren't just drivin'. I told myself not to turn 'round, I told myself to keep walkin' forward.

I only had about a mile left of my walk, but it was too far to outrun any kind of car. I assumed I was screwed either way, there wasn't much I could do besides act tough.

"Millie?" a voice called out. "I've been looking for you everywhere".

I coulda picked his voice out from a line of however many. *Colton.* He pulled up in his red and four-doored chevy, and I asked him what he was doin' here lookin' fer me. He put his truck in park and got out quicker than a rabbit meetin' its match.

"I met up with Abilene after school and she told me you'd been walkin' on the days she couldn't drive you. Is that true?".

"What's it to you?" I asked.

He towered over me, pinchin' his lips into a flat line before leanin' on his truck to relax a bit.

"What's it to me? It's everything" his lips relaxed. "Just ask and I'll bring you home".

"You're always busy" I joined him, leanin' on his truck. "I don't wanna ask you to take time off fer me".

He put a hand on my shoulder and it felt different, not wrong, nor did it make my body shake. It made me weak, heart heavy, and face warm. His hands slipped 'round my back and they took the heavy bag I was carryin' off my shoulders.

I watched as light rained down and out from the swayin' leaves of branches that covered the sun in the crisp month and amber pools poured from his honey eyes.

His full lips smirked and he dropped his head to the dirt road. I wanted to reach up and move a piece of his sandy brown hair from his eyes.

But I didn't, cause if I did, it would mean things would change. I didn't know if he even wanted that with me, I was pretty blind to those kinds of things. Actually, I was full on blind to everythin' regardin' the birds and the bees. Mama never taught me, I never taught myself.

Everythin' I knew, I learned from Abilene and what she told me with the boyfriends she had. Everyone liked her, she was the cute girl down the block; energetic, outgoin', extrovert, and loved to party.

But I? I was not like her at all. That's what made us the perfect peas to God's little pod.

"I'm never too busy for you" he opened the side door. "C'mon, it's Friday night and I've got work off. Let's go see an outdoor movie or somethin', we can pick up Abilene too. I doubt she's busy".

"Just tell her Brooks is there and she'll go" I let him help me in.

"I'll tell Brooks she's going and he'll be there too" he joked.

We drove with the windows down, country music blastin' on the radio. Colton took too many wrongs turns to get me home in a quick manner, but it was okay; I wasn't afraid like I'd been with Hunter.

We drove past corn fields and other farm lands, and though I panicked slightly inside my fire-lit brain, it only lasted a second. Colton was safe. I smiled cause his singin' grew louder, and it was terrible.

"Wow" I laughed. "You really are tone-deaf".

He said nothin', simply smiled, turned up the radio, and continued on singin' his tunes. It was like he was tryin' to cheer me up from somethin' he knew and I didn't. Maybe he knew what Hunter did to me.

He knew all about daddy and how mama felt from him takin' me. Maybe he knew about Hunter too.

We pulled into my driveway and he helped me loosen the broken buckle to my seat. I asked him to wait in the truck fer me to get changed and ready myself fer the movie. It was gonna be a cold night, so I had to dress warmly.

Colton was a sweet southern boy; he had no problems waitin' fer me while I got ready. He'd been in my house a million times, still, today and the past few months were different. Things were different between us and I had an education to focus on that involved myself and I.

I acted cool until I got inside, that's when I turned the entire trailer inside out tryin' to find my best clothes. Abilene told me I should dress nicely fer the boy I liked, which she knew was Colton. She knew before I even had the chance to tell her.

Turns out, bein' poor meant I didn't have a lot of nice things to dress myself in. I washed my face in the sink and tried not to sulk at my reflection. I'd been called a pretty girl my entire life, yet starin' at myself, I never felt like it.

I let down my hair from the bun it'd been in all day and my hair was set in loose curls. I quickly brushed my teeth and threw on a pair of jeans with a black long sleeve. I added my favorite blue and green flannel, and to bottom it off, my tan boots.

I looked at the microwave clock and jumped in my skin, I'd kept him waitin' fer almost fifteen minutes. I knew my stomach was gonna be mad at me later fer not eatin' but I didn't have time.

I grabbed a few blankets from the couch, givin' them a good sniff, and I threw them back down. Nothin' was good usin' to share. I left everythin' behind and grabbed a small bag to hold the few dollars I owned and the flip phone mama got me last year.

As soon as I got outside, a cold breeze hit me and I knew I'd be freezin' before the movie began. Still, I held my breath to stop the shiverin' and I got back into his truck, not wantin' to cause him more of a worry.

"Sorry" I looked away embarrassed. "I was lookin' fer somethin' but couldn't find it".

"Millie" his voice was breathless. "You look amazing".

"Yeah?" I tried to match his tone.

"Like a real shinny penny I found last week in the parkin' lot" he said in a loud and sarcastic tone, copyin' all the rednecks' accents. "Yee-haw, we better get goin' if we're gonna make it to the debutante ball now, princess".

"Oh, shut up" I gave him a push.

We threw jokes at each other like we had a stick and a sleepin' bear to poke at as we drove to his house. I guess he talked to Brooks while I was gettin' ready and he said Brooks already got Abe. They were gonna get some food together beforehand.

We parked just outside his daddy's garage, close to the stairs of the front porch. His house was a decent size; three bedrooms and two bathrooms. Their front yard was large and had a nice oak in the front where we used to tie ropes to and swing from 'em.

"Wait here" he smiled, shutttin' me in.

I popped up from my seat and watched as he waked 'round the front of the truck and met me at my door. He opened it up and told me to watch my step as he helped me down. I hid my smile as best as I could and took his hand fer balance.

I immediately let go the moment I saw his little sister starin' from the front window. He looked back at her and stuck out his tongue as if to say she were in trouble and she quickly ducked behind the curtains. Ever since I met her, Cheryl was always a menace.

I walked into the warm home, fillin' my nose with apple and cinnamon, which led me to the kitchen. Colton said hi to his mama who was cookin' applesauce on the stove. I said my hello's to her and Cheryl, and she asked if I was stayin' fer dinner.

Virginia was a beautiful woman. She was tall, had thick dark red hair, and freckles you'd think were the stars. Her voice was sweet like honey and anyone could've easily fallen asleep to her lullaby of a voice.

"Of course, how could we say no to your delicious cooking?" Colton smiled before leavin' to his room to shower up and change.

I walked back to the front door and took off my shoes and flannel while thinkin' he must've known I skipped my meals today and hadn't eaten since yesterday's lunch.

Maybe he heard my stomach growlin' in the car? I thought I hadn't been so loud.

Their kitchen opened up into the livin' room and I joined Cheryl on the couch. I could still see their mama cookin' in the kitchen through the half wall that divided the two rooms. Despite her femininity, Cheryl looked more like Colton than she did her own mama.

"How you been?" his mama, Virginia, smiled warmly. "How's school been? I heard you're doin' public school fer your last year".

I told her everythin' I knew she wanted to hear, while leavin' out a few details. Public school sucked and she agreed with me, wishin' she could homeschool Cheryl but she was too busy with work. I told her how I was top of my class, but so was Colton, so I didn't expect the praise she gave me.

I left out the bits that included Hunter and the parts that practically screamed I liked her son, though I feared she already knew that part.

I smiled while she talked because of the advice she gave and her accent. Not only was her name Virginia, but she was born there as well. I guess her mama had a thing for namin' kids where they were born. Colton once told me his aunt, her sister, was named and born in one of the Carolinas.

Cheryl cut in here and there to tell me I was doin' everythin' wrong. She said I should doll myself up more, get a fake pair of hoo-ha's, and find myself a rich man. She was startin' to sound a lot like my mama.

"I just wanna be a mom" she looked at hers. "I wanna have at least twelve kids, a rich husband so I never have to lift a finger, and I wanna have a pool in my house, with lots of goats runnin' 'round".

"How ambitious" Virginia laughed. "How about you go tell your brother dinner is ready".

"Honestly, mama, that just sounds like too much work fer me right now" she pretended to sleep.

"You better wake up and start workin' if you want all those children and goats runnin' 'round" I whispered, but she didn't budge. "I'll go let him know dinner is done, anythin' else I can help you with?".

"That girl is gonna round me tighter than a clock one of these days if she hasn't already" Virginia laughed. "It's okay, sweetie. Just go on and tell Colton foods ready".

His room was just down the hall and to the left, away from most of the home's noises. Just as I was to knock, I saw him through the creek in the door. He was shirtless and wore a pair of dark jeans.

His hair was still wet and the shower's dew dripped down his face and strong chest. I hadn't realized the amount of muscle he put on since joinin' the police academy. I swallowed hard and closed my eyes; he was no longer a boy, but rather, a man.

I raised my hand, but I was too late. He already caught me starin', already saw the blush on my face, and he snickered to himself because of it. He opened the door and pulled me in, wrappin' a warm hand 'round the lower part of my back.

I put my hands up to keep some distance, but he closed it and my fingers were now grazin' the skin on his chest. I raised them up to cover my mouth and his eyes stared deeply into mine. I couldn't look away, even if I wanted to, I couldn't escape his rough gaze.

"Uh-the food" I stuttered and dropped my head. "It's done".

He lifted my head with the tip of his finger and I followed willingly. I was caught in his look like a moth flyin' to the moon, unable to go anywhere else. He whispered my name and began to lean in towards my lips.

My hands fell back to his chest and I clenched and unclenched my fists as he made way fer me. I prayed I wouldn't freak out. It was somethin' I wanted, somethin' I wanted fer a real long time. Yet, I didn't deserve it.

Hunter once did that to me; he once did a lot more. How was I goin' to be kissed when all I saw was the face of someone I never wanted to see? The same face I would rather claw out my eyes with a crow's beak than to face once more.

To save myself from somethin' I didn't want savin' from, I quickly ran from his room and slowed down a bit until joinin' his sister and mama at the dinin' table. I told her I told him and I took to my usual spot, across from his mama and next to his chair.

Colton entered fully dressed just seconds later and I avoided his gaze as we ate what his mama made. I always felt bad eatin' without bringin' anythin' in return. Mama got mad whenever I ate at his house, said Virginia was makin' fun of us fer bein' poor.

She'd always make me walk to the store and buy some kind of dessert to bring. Virginia always smiled and took whatever I gave her, puttin' it on the table, and swallowin' a piece down. I think mama was wrong, and that Virginia just wanted the company since her husband was always workin'.

We finished our food by the time it took fer the sky to set and the stars to say goodnight in a way the sun would say hello. Colton asked if I was ready and I said yes, joinin' him by puttin' on my shoes and flannel. He grabbed a handful of blankets from the small linen closet in the hall and returned.

"I hope to see you soon, Millie" Virginia called out. "Have your mom call me too! I haven't talked to her in such a long time".

"I will. Thank you again, Virginia".

Colton didn't say anythin' when we got in his truck, neither did I when we pulled out of the driveway and headed towards the outdoor movie theater. He didn't turn on the music, roll the windows down, and he didn't even sing.

"Are you-" I didn't bother finishin' my question.

We stayed silent fer an hour in my mind. I played with my thumbs and started pickin' at my nails like I was a dog back in its kennel. Colton placed a gentle hand over mine and he gave me a pitied smile.

"I'm sorry for how I acted" he sighed. "I shouldn't have done that".

I wondered if he regretted tryin' to kiss me because it was me. I wondered if he was mad at himself for tryin' to kiss someone like me.

"I like you, Millie. But I shouldn't have assumed you liked me the same way" he let go of my hand.

I wanted to be brave like him, *romantic*. How Abilene told me to be, but I just couldn't reach back fer his hand. I was a coward, somethin' I'd have to get used to.

"Don't be sorry" I said monotoned. "It's not like I didn't want you to not do it. I just think I need some time".

What was I even spittin' and goin' on about?

He said nothin' but smiled to himself like I wasn't watchin'. We even got all the way to the drive-in without him sayin' a single word. We parked next to Brooks and I helped Colton set up the back of his truck after he dropped down the tailgate.

I hadn't noticed it before, but he put a pad in the back fer us so it wouldn't be hard fer our bodies to lay on. I gave Abilene a hug and she batted her eyes and looked back and forth between Colton and I.

"Okay, somethin' definitely happened between y'all. Spit it out" she dragged me to the concession stand.

"He tried to kiss me, but I was dumb and pulled away" I declined the candy she offered me. "That was it".

"Oh no, somethin' is definitely wrong" she spoke soft and dramatically. "Ya just denied yer favorite, snickers".

"Abe, this is serious" I smacked her hand away. "I don't want things to be awkward now".

"This is worse fer Colton" she laughed. "Poor guy just prolly had his entire world shatter before his eyes".

"What do you mean?" I followed her towards the trucks. "Abilene, answer me".

"Dude's got it hard fer ya. Thought ya knew that" she took a bite of her twizzler and jumped into the back of Brooks's truck.

Colton helped me into the back of his and a sense of guilt washed over me. I didn't let him do somethin' he wanted, and for that, I felt stupid. Even though it was somethin' I didn't mind as well, I was just too stuck in the past to get.

I sat on the opposite side of the makeshift bed, away from Colton. I wasn't even payin' attention to the horror movie I was too afraid to watch. All I could think about was how close he got to me earlier, how he trapped me between him and the wall.

I waved a hand 'round the inside of my head to try and swat away the flies that were shittin' scat over my thoughts, but it was fer no use at all. I brought my knees to my chest and shivered in the cold breeze that occasionally dipped down.

"Millie" Colton whispered. "It's a lot warmer over here".

He opened the blankets to show there was warmth and room on his side, but I ignored him. He let out a deep sigh and I heard him shift in the sheets. Before I had time to protest, he grabbed me by the waist and pulled me against him.

He wrapped the blankets 'round our bodies and let my head fall over his arm, the other hand over my waist. I froze, my heart didn't beat, and my eyes didn't blink. There were no thoughts besides hundreds of busy bees whisperin' different words in my ear that I couldn't understand.

"Is this okay?' he whispered in my ear.

I nodded twice and the sound of his heart beatin' heavily against my chest brought mine back to life. I told myself not to freak out, I told myself I was okay. The last time I had been in a similar position was involuntarily, without my consent, and it wasn't with Hunter.

It was only two years ago, though my memory is still a little fuzzy on this one. I just couldn't believe the audacity she had after.

I was in her room, Trish's room, holdin' her brand new baby. Her boyfriend had just gotten outta the shower, thankfully changin' in the bathroom. Trish left me alone with her boyfriend and their newborn.

He came close to me, I kept my eyes on the new life, tellin' his daddy how he can't see color yet. His daddy didn't care. He put his hand on my braids and told me he liked em', rubbin' them with his thumb. I looked at his baby, never up.

He put a hand on my inner thigh and squeezed, movin' his way up, until I began to squirm. I told him again that his baby could only see shapes and not actual people yet.

"Look up" the monster demanded and I listened.

He placed his free hand on my shoulder and held me firm against the wall while usin' his other to pin my thigh in place. He brought his lips close to mine and I asked him why without words.

"What the hell" I got up and he let go. "You need to tell Trish, no I'll tell her, should we tell her together?".

He sat on the bed next to me and I gently handed him his baby. I stormed outta the small room and into the livin' room, where her mama, sister, and her were.

"I'm leavin' you can talk to yer boyfriend about what he did" I gave her no time to ask questions.

I immediately went home and took out my braids, jumpin' into the shower before it was warm, and before I could even get my clothes off. I felt disgusted, violated.

I got out and the house phone rang when we still had one, it was Trish. She asked me to come back, said her boyfriend explained everythin' and left the house. Like the idiot I was, I went back to her after changin' my clothes.

We both laid on her bed while her mama soothed our cries. After a moment, she asked me to go lookin' fer him with her, and I stupidly said yes. I sat in the back of the truck with their baby boy as we searched the back roads, finally findin' him.

She dropped him off at his mama's house, leavin' me outside with the baby while she talked with him fer an hour, then she came back out. She took her baby from me and went back inside fer an extra hour again, until she drove me back home.

He told her she wasn't givin' him enough, even though she just had a kid. There was more to the story, and Trish even asked me not to tell anyone after *everythin' that happened. He's a piece of trash and no better than flies eatin' shit, and sometimes, I think she is too for askin' me to keep quiet.*

Soon, the soft screams of movie characters meetin' their death became a sweet lullaby in the realm of my dreams. The calm heart of the one that held me close was no match for my mind in stayin' awake. I was fallin' asleep, fast, and hard, I couldn't help myself.

"I can wait forever if it means I get to be by your side" he kissed the top of my head, thinkin' I was out like a light.

And I was, but not before then. That was the last thing I remembered, the warmth of his lips caressin' my soul into believin' it was safe forever and always would be. It caressed the traumas done to my body, bid farewell, and promised peace and security fer the rest of my days to come.

Oh how wrong I was.

CHAPTER IV

Months passed since I last felt okay. Seein' Hunter umpteen spiraled my anxiety when I knew it shouldn't have. No matter how hard I tried, I just couldn't get over what he did to me, or what the others tried.

I sounded like a broken record whenever I tried to fix what happened in my head, but at some point, I stopped listenin' to myself. It didn't matter anymore, nothin' really did. I was just tryin' to get through the last few months of school by keepin' my head down.

Stay invisible, they can't see you there.

I figured I'd get a job after graduatin', prolly at the gas station or small convenience store until I could save up enough money fer a car. I think I'd prolly quit my job and get a better one in the next town over, makin' more too.

Mama wanted me to go to college, not many people in this town went. I think she thought it'd help me jump some metaphorical ladder and I'd automatically be successful. I knew I was smart, but that was only in this town. Out there, in the real world, I was the short end of the stick kinda gal.

It didn't really work fer me, keepin' my head down, stayin' silent, and whatnot. I think Abilene was gettin' a little sick of me and how wish-wash I was with plans. She seemed kinda like a party girl now, and her school friends didn't care to have me tag along.

I finished washin' my hands in the bathroom, takin' my time to fix the sweat smeared makeup Abilene done to my face. It was her birthday after all, so I couldn't say no. There were too many people at her house fer my likin', I reckoned the whole school came to party.

Everyone liked her parties. We'd take our trucks deep into the back of her woods and have a bonfire with booze and music playin'. Not this time though, it was too cold fer that. We parked our bodies inside the warm house, it was easy too, since her parents left town fer the week.

"How long is Millie gonna stay fer" a voice asked.

I paused my steps and waited behind the archway of the kitchen, eavesdroppin' on the conversation.

"What's it matter to ya?" Abe asked.

"Oh, don't make that face Abilene. Ya know we love ya, but Millie is kinda weird".

"Yeah, she's too quiet, makes everythin' akward".

"Listen" Abilene spoke softly. "I know she's a clodhopper, but what can I do? She's a sister to me and I'm not gonna kick her out cause all y'all's gotta problem with her".

I carefully turned 'round and headed fer the livin' room, but someone caught me. I knew by his scent who he was before I got a good look at his face. I said nothin' and neither did he. He simply took me by the hand and walked me into the small and quiet library Abilene's mama insisted on buildin'.

It was a small and dark room, with a few brown bookshelves, dark patterned carpet, and blue walls. Abilene's mama called it 'art', I called it 'too much'. I *straightened my back and sat on the small bench in front of the only window. It outlooked the crisp and bare forest.*

"You're not a clodhopper" Colton joined me on the bench.

I tensed as his shoulder touched mine, and I told myself I was a fool fer thinkin' about the trauma. Colton wasn't gonna hurt me, and if he did, it'd just be another name to add to the list. There were more names, I knew that.

I just couldn't remember who they were. My brain liked to dissociate whenever it was happenin', there was nothin' I could do. I was never strong enough, loud enough, or even just simply good enough to stop what was happenin' to me.

"Millie?" Colton put a hand on my leg, but quickly drew it back. "I'm sorry. I didn't mean-".

"It's okay" I faked a smile because I prayed too many times to know it wasn't.

"Pay no attention to what those girls said about you. Honestly, they probably just don't like how close you are to Abe".

"Yeah" was all I could say. "I'm sure you're right" I knew he was wrong.

"Besides" he looked my way and smiled, just inches from my face and I forgot how to breathe. "I like you, Abe likes you, and don't get me started on how much my mama and Cheryl wish you were their family instead of me".

I kept quiet, didn't wanna disturb the moment my mind finally settled. It was like a river flooded my brain and pushed away pebbles without me havin' to do anythin'. I took a deep breath in and out and relaxed my back so it could slouch.

"Are you okay, Mil?".

"No" I whispered. "But I couldn't tell you why".

We stayed in that room like we'd been locked in all night. We never said anythin' after that, never even spoke so much as a whisper. I started cryin' at one point and he just held me like he knew all the secrets I'd never tell.

I sat on a cold bench with Abe and her friends, watchin' the last football game of the season. I was shiverin' in the thick sweater and jeans I had on. Abe shared a blanket with her girlfriends, I didn't bother askin' if I could join, they would've made some excuse reasonin' why I couldn't.

I was the smallest of them all, if anythin', they were too big. Still, it was my fault fer not thinkin' it would've been colder than usual on a Friday night. I wished Colton were there, cause I knew he'd give me the last shirt off his back to keep me warm, even though I'd never ask.

"How much longer is left of the game?" I asked.

"If she didn't wanna watch, she shouldn't have come" one of the girls whispered.

"Millie, can ya get me a slice of pizza?" Abilene fished a five dollar from her bag. "I don't wanna miss anythin', especially if Brooks scores".

"Yeah" I smiled, takin' the money from her.

Really, I just didn't care to watch and I didn't care to sit like a puppy dog on a leash listenin' to her friends. When I stood up and walked away, I heard Abe reprimandin' them on my behalf, callin' them rude and inconsiderate. I didn't feel bad fer the earful they were gettin'.

I made way to the concession stand positioned between the field and forestry, eager to see the line was long. I wanted to take my time gettin' back to Abe, and this gave me the perfect excuse.

I was only about a few feet from the last person in line when hands covered my mouth and dragged me into the woods. I couldn't scream, kick, or punch. I weighed the same as a large dog and was no taller than a kid.

My heart was beatin' so fast it didn't know what to do, even my eyes didn't cry. I was completely dissociated from it all. Knowin' I would never remember any of it, I begged them through their fingers that covered my mouth to stop.

"Whachu' sayin?" hot breath laughed in my ear. "You gonna like this, I promise".

Dear God, if any prayers are to be answered I scream and beg of you to make it stop this time. God, please help me in this time of urgency.

The man slipped his hands down the front of my pants and I finally cried. Tears began to pour down my face, so much so, my face freed and I was able to scream fer a second before coverin' it back up. He started slippin' off my pants while doin' the same to his and I blacked out.

Say it was me, God, or whoever, I just couldn't remember. I stared at the trees, rememberin' that God had a purpose, that God had a plan. I couldn't even ask why it had to be like that fer me. All I could do was pray fer intervention, no matter the costs.

It seemed like days, weeks, and months passed in my head. I was alone, floatin' in a black abyss without anyone, anythin', and I was nowhere to be found. I think there were other footsteps in the woods. I think someone else was with us.

That's when I knew, God answered, but not how I thought. Instead of sendin' one of his guardian angels, he sent the fallen one. The devil who paraded 'round, wearin' the halo of a saint. *Hunter.* I thought I was a goner, that they'd share me like a meal.

And I was wrong.

Hunter said nothin' as he approached us, even the guy didn't hear him cause he was focused on *other* things. I could hardly see cause there wasn't much light, but my God was he furious. It was like someone had stolen his favorite toy.

"What the hell do ya think yer doin' to my girl" he whispered close.

My attacker finally realized what was happenin', so he fixed his pants and ran off. I stared at the forest floor, tryin' to get me to come back, but I was out of it. I said hello to my thoughts, but they never so much as sent me an echo back.

I heard the sharp pain of a slap to the face, but I didn't dare turn around. There was fumblin' goin' 'round like two animals fightin' fer the same prey. Grunts of heavy breathin' rolled near, so much so, I saw what was happenin' in front of me.

I watched the silhouette of Hunter sittin' on the man, he was beatin' his face in with a rock. I knew I'd be in bigger trouble if I stayed, so I fixed myself on wobblin' legs and stood leanin' on a tree.

"If you tell anyone about this, I'll have to kill ya" Hunter turned his head with a crooked smile and I believed him.

I pressed my lips into a flat line and quickly turned fer the field. *What just happened?* I held onto my throbbin' head and ran as fast as I could outta there. It was like watchin' a movie in reverse, only I couldn't remember any of it.

I tried focusin' on pictures, words, what I felt, heard, and seen, but there was nothin'. I cussed at my body and mind for wantin' to forget. I wasn't gonna say anythin' to no one, they'd never believe me. I wasn't gonna do nothin' bad with it, I just wanted to know fer myself.

"Where's my pizza?".

I was already sittin' back in my seat when I came to my senses. I avoided Abilene's gaze cause I knew it meant I'd have to lie straight to her face again. This way, I could lie to the side of her face instead.

"Jesus, Millie, did you run through a mud track?" she grabbed onto my face.

I looked at my dirt covered hands and wiped them on my sweater before pullin' my face back from her. My eyes were stingin' too from holdin' in the pain of lyin' to my best friend. I wanted to tell her everythin', I wanted to trust her enough to tell her everythin'.

"I fell" I watched the game.

"Don't think we ain't gonna talk about this later, missy" she whispered in my ear.

I had nothin' to say to her, the world 'round me started goin' blank. It was gettin' quiet, tired, darker. I felt myself loosin' myself. So I sat there, like nothin' happened, because it didn't.

Because nothin' happened.

I made it all up.

***

They put balloons up all 'round town. Some guy went missin', but I reckon it was fer good reason. The bridge rails, street lamp posts, trees, and home fences were all decorated in blue balloons, missin' posters, and a phone number to call if you had any information regardin' his disappearance.

"I can't believe Timothys missin'; it ain't like him" Shelby Ann said to my right.

I reckon she was the bastard's girlfriend, *poor thing*. He'd only been discovered missin' since Saturday morn' when no one could get 'hold of him. It'd only been two days. Shelby Ann let out another cry and her friend tried consolin' her, but them little white tissues kept bein' pulled from the box.

"Are ya kiddin' me? Tim prolly got drunk Friday night and again on Saturday. He knows his mama woulda given him an arse whoopin' if he came home trashed" Curtis laughed. "If I were him, I'd lay low too".

The teacher told everyone to settle down and then we prayed fer him, the missin' man that apparently everyone *loved* and knew so well. Most prayers were silent, but there were some people that whispered theirs aloud.

Abilene took her prayer time serious, but I knew she wasn't askin' God about Timothy Handerthorn. She was prolly prayin' about Brooks and the broken rib he got Friday night from his team's victory win. I rolled my eyes and Mrs. McGuire gave me a dauntin' stare, my head quicky fell to my hands.

Dear God, I pray in your favor that Timothy be found with a serious concussion and no memory of what he did to me. I pray Shelby Ann breaks up with his sorry butt and she finds herself a nice man. Lastly, I pray that they ain't servin' mystery meat again fer lunch.

With each class I attended, I felt myself question if anythin' happened after all. Everyone told priceless stories of Tim that made everyone laugh, cry, and say "that's our Tim". If I hadn't known any better, I woulda said he was a good guy.

Made me wonder what actually happened to him, but I knew someone who could tell me. So when the last bell rang, I quickly packed up my things and walked outside. I froze in my tracks, stuck like a fly in honey when the cold air hit my lungs.

There had to have been at least seven police cars scattered throughout. They had dogs too and were searchin' for any traces of him. Each one was in the wrong spot; each crew had no clue where anythin' was.

"Weird, huh?" a cold voice creeped up my spine.

He put his arm 'round my shoulder and told me he was drivin' me home. I didn't wanna go nowhere with him, just wanted some answers. I looked up at him and he smiled like he wasn't a psychopath, almost like we were *friends*.

The police started gettin' closer to the school, even started askin' students if they knew anythin'. I couldn't let them talk to me. I woulda thought with all the years of lyin' to mama and my friends that I'd be solid lyin' to a cop, but that ain't the case.

The police couldn't help me either. Why would I tell 'em of Timothy, but not Hutner? Why wouldn't I have told them about Trish's boyfriend? There ain't nothin' that can be done about it. Especially now that I'm older and have his arm wrapped 'round my shoulder.

Sometimes I wonder if I made it all up in my head, *maybe it never happened.*

I took a gamble and audibly sighed, followin' him to his car. I didn't want nothin' to do with him, and I kept tellin' myself I could always run home if he tried anythin' on me. Abilene couldn't take me home anyway, and I didn't wanna inconvenience Colton since I knew he had work later.

I willingly got in Hunter's truck and I think it surprised him just as much as it did me. He asked if I was warm enough and I told him to just take me home. It started snowin' about half way home and neither of us spoke a word to each other.

It wasn't strange fer me to be like that, but fer Hunter, it wasn't normal. I played with my fingers and counted to ten in my head. I told myself when I got to ten I'd ask him what he did. When ten came 'round, I did ten more, and more after that. I got to eighty-nine when I was just about to ask.

"What do ya remember?" he spoke.

"What did you do to him?" I asked at the same time.

He sighed and pulled over to the side of the road and I put my hand on the door's handle, preparin' myself fer anythin' that coulda happened. He kept his head down and took his own turn starin' at his hands.

"I ain't gonna hurt ya, Millie, so ya can take ya damn hand off that there handle. I thought ya would've forgotten it" he rolled up his sleeves, showin' torn and bruised skin.

"What did you do?" I asked again.

"He was hurtin' ya" he met my gaze, eyes glossed over. "He was doin' nasty things to ya, Millie. I couldn't let him do that to ya, so I did what needed to be done".

"Where is he?" I tried to act calm. "Is he okay?".

I changed my prayer; *Dear God, I pray he's alive. I pray I ain't one of them people that gets in trouble fer someone else's recklessness. Dear God, I pray he's alive and doesn't remember.*

"You're not gonna tell on me, are ya?" he rotated towards me and my back hit the door. "I really hope you'll let this be our little secret".

Blurry pictures floated in front of my eyes like I was experiencin' my time with Timothy all over again. All the disgustin' and horror-filled things he did while the whole school sat not even half a mile away. Abilene never asked me more about that night, or the dirt on my body like she said she was gonna.

I remembered prayin' fer somethin' or anyone to put a stop to it, and that's when Hunter showed up. I wondered if that's who God wanted fer me at that time. I had to be just as crazy.

"Thank you" I whispered.

His brows furrowed and his lips spoke words I couldn't hear. He looked distraught or some type of confused that was incomprehensible. I told him again thank you and he sat back in his chair with a genuine smile on his lips.

He knew he won; cause I wasn't gonna tell no one. If I did, I'd have to tell em' all about what I was doin' there with him in the first place. Even worse, I'd have to tell em' why Hunter stepped in, and that, ain't ever gonna be an option.

I sat back in my chair and he started again takin' me home. I didn't say nothin', just assumed he beat the guy, with a rock, over the head, and maybe I was in the car with a serial killer. A serial killer that did it to protect me. I was an accomplice to his crimes; I was the reason fer his crimes.

It was my fault.

We got to the start of the driveway when Hunter stopped. He told me he wouldn't drive all the way up cause he knew I didn't like it. I kinda just stopped what I was doin' and stared right at him. He was still varmint, inside and out, and he was bein' too nice to me.

Just as I reached fer the door's handle, he grabbed my arm and pulled me close. Our faces were just inches apart and I tried to push myself away from him, but he was too strong.

He stared at me, all of me. Felt like he was undressin' me with his eyes fer hours before he finally moved his yapper.

"I did it fer ya, Millie" he squeezed me tight and I winced. "I don't wanna, but I'll kill ya too if ya tell anyone about this. Ya know that, right?".

I nodded just once and he let me go. I quickly opened the door and began my run up the driveway, slippin' on new snow and the fear that I was forever indebted to him. Mama was waitin' outside in a faux fur coat fer me on the makeshift porch when I finally reached our trailer.

"Millie Maye, don't tell me you walked all the way home in this here weather?" she crossed her arms over her chest.

"Of course not, mama" I smiled and gave her a hug. "Abilene didn't have a lot of time, so I told her to drop me off at the end of the drive".

"You better not be lyin' to me".

I followed her into the house and it wasn't much warmer. I reckoned it was time to start choppin' wood and bringin' it in. I took in a deep breath and held it fer a long time before lettin' it go. It was my way of stayin' calm.

"I don't want you endin' up like that boy from yer school" mama said. "I can't even begin to imagine what they must be feelin' right now. They don't even know where their son is. I'd much rather wanna know if he was dead or not instead of havin' to guess".

"You have nothin' to worry about" I lied again, swallowin' a lump in my throat.

You have every reason to fear fer me, mama.

CHAPTER V

Time went by too slow. I ain't poetic, but if I could describe it, it'd be somethin' like; time was a dark mystery to me, and I was drownin' in it.

Weeks went by, even months, and they still hadn't found Timothy's body. Abilene and Brooks were real serious and we all suspected he'd propose after graduation'. I was envious of her, I wanted everythin' she had; nice house with her ma and pa, lovin' boyfriend, and good looks.

I could only see Colton once every week cause of his schedule, and even then, things were awkward between us, but that was my fault. He tried kissin' me again and I freaked out, I don't think he'll ever try again.

In the dead of winter, we cozied up on the couch at his house. His mama, daddy, and sister were all outta town helpin' his daddy with somethin'. I didn't really care to ask about what cause it gave us time alone.

His skin smelt like evergreen trees and sap, even his hair locked in the same invitin' scents of winter and smoke from the stove outside. The tv wasn't big, but I didn't care, it was just another excuse to get closer to him.

I curled up into a ball next to him and rest my head on his shoulder, he wrapped an arm 'round me, even put a hand on my knee. I tensed when he did that and he quickly took it off, but I told him it was okay and lied sayin' his hands were cold. I knew he knew somethin' was up with me, and I prayed he wouldn't ask about it.

I didn't even know what we were watchin' cause I was too busy thinkin' about how close we were, what could happen, where it was goin'. I was thinkin' about them guys that decided fer me, the ones that took my vote away.

He turned toward me and I stupidly looked at his full lips. They smiled, smirked, and then came closer. I didn't know what to do, I leaned in, remembered their faces, then leaned back. Finally, I made an audible sound that pushed him away.

His lips pinched to a flat line and I wanted to reach out and tell him I was sorry, I wanted to tell him I wanted it too. But I couldn't say nothin', and so we sat watchin' the movie in a silence that pierced my ears and wasn't real.

"Millie" Colton lowered the volume and turned towards me. "Are you okay?",

"What do ya mean?" I played pretend.

"Do I make you uncomfortable?".

My thoughts screamed no, but I couldn't say it on my lips. He took his arm off my shoulder and nodded like I had given him his answer. I didn't move, I froze there like them icicles hangin' from the roof.

"I'll get you some tea" he pushed aside the blanket and got up.

I prepared a very good speech in my head fer when he got back. I was gonna tell him I liked him, that he didn't make me nervous, that I was just inexperienced and didn't know what to do, that I got somethin' wrong with me, and more.

But by the time he came back, my words had already run away. He handed me the warm cup, tellin' me to be careful and he sat back down, further from me. I knew if I didn't say nothin', then nothin' was ever gonna happen, so I bit my pride just as he turned up the volume.

"No" it was a whisper.

"No?" he echoed.

"You don't make me uncomfortable" I played with the tea bag. "You're the only guy that doesn't, and I feel like I can be myself 'round you. I think I want what you want, but I dunno where we stand sometimes and I ain't good at recognizin' cues".

"I like you" he turned with a smile on his lips.

I couldn't say nothin' to that, just hoped it was obvious by me hidin' my face in the mug that I liked him too. It was kinda awkward after that, no one said anythin' until the movie came to an end and it was just them credits playin' in the background.

"Can I ask you something?" I jumped at his voice.

"What is it?".

"Wh-Who hurt you?" he stared at me and I couldn't face him. "I want you to know you can tell me anything. I'm here 100 percent for you".

"No one" I lied. "No one hurt me".

"Millie-" he reached fer my hands.

"I said no one, okay? No one hurt me" my voice was way higher than it shoulda been.

I was rewatchin' what they did to me. I was rememberin' their voices, rememberin' their faces. I was rewatchin' everythin' I forgot happened to me. It overcame me like a floodin' river, but I didn't cry. I was like the desert; selfish.

"I prolly made it all up, they weren't real, they did nothin' to me, okay? I didn't do nothin', it wasn't my fault" I was hysterical.

"It's okay" he wrapped my arms across my chest then held me tight with his chest pressed against my back. "You don't have to explain anything".

"It wasn't my fault" I was like a child cryin' cause their toy got taken away.

I knew he was sayin' more to me, I knew he was squeezin' me tighter, tryin' to take away my panicked breath. It was no use though, cause I couldn't breathe no more, couldn't see no more too. I remember everythin' slowly turnin' off, without askin' if anyone was still there.

Next thing I knew, I woke up in his bed the followin' day. He slept on the couch, made me breakfast, and told me I could talk to him about anythin'. Said he'd keep my secrets as his, and then he drove me home.

I got a butt whoopin' from mama later, told me I scared her senseless without so much as a call to tell her I was alright.

So time went by, and I felt I was indebted to Hunter. I let him drive me home, even let him take me to the park three times. Each time, he made a basket with food and drinks. I barely touched the stuff, I just wanted outta there.

He had anger issues. Had a conniption fit and told me I was bein' ungrateful, that I should give him more of me than just my presence cause of everythin' he done fer me. I never said anythin' when he talked like that, only told him he was hurtin' me when he grabbed my arm too hard sometimes.

He never tried touchin' me again like that one-day years ago, still made me wonder if all of it was made up, just a nightmare I had when I was a dumb kid. I started wonderin' if I was actually just imaginin' everythin' bad that happened to me. Maybe none of it was real and I was just psychotic.

That's why I never told Colton anythin' other than what my ramblin' mouth said that one night at his house when I ended up passin' out. I didn't wanna lie to him, but what if my truth was still a lie, but I just didn't know it?

I ain't sure of really anythin' anymore. All I knew was to keep my days with Hunter private from the rest of the world, and I think that ended up hurtin' me more in the end cause of his *fit*. I also didn't want Colton and Abe thinkin' there was more goin' on between us, cause there sure as hell wasn't and I'll be damned to let others think there were.

I felt like it wasn't a big deal too, since he was pretty MIA for a while. I actually hadn't seen him in about a hot month. Once every blue moon, but not every white.

I guess it was my mistake fer not speakin' up sooner, but I didn't know.

"Millie!" Abilene ran over after parkin' her car somewhere off.

It was already summer, school permanently ended not even eight hours ago and we were already celebratin'. Mama didn't know what I was doin', I lied and told her I was just gonna stay home and read a book. It was a good lie, since she was workin' another double.

I sat on the back of someone's tailgate, lookin' up at the stars, not even sure of who's truck I was even on. There were a few more of em' around us, kinda makin' a circle with a big fire in the middle. Someone had drinks and stuff in the back of one, and another had hotdogs and whatever you needed to make em'.

"Hey Abe, hey Brooks" I smiled at the approachin' pair.

I was relieved to see 'em come since I didn't really know anyone and their numbers stared growin'. I started seein' upperclassmen who already graduated comin' in, and younger kids from classes below. I looked 'round fer Colton, but couldn't find him amongst anyone.

"He's comin' in about thirty" Brooks smiled.

"Who?" I asked like I didn't know.

"You're funny, ya know that?" Abilene smiled. "Brooks, can you give us a little girl time?".

He helped her up into the bed of the truck, gave her a long kiss, and smiled as he walked away. Yup, I was definitely jealous of the lack of control she had to be so free like that with a guy. We talked about how we felt now that school was over, what we were gonna do, and I told her I didn't know.

"I kinda know" she smiled, holdin' up her left hand to show a shinin' diamond on her finger. "He asked me not long ago and I said yes".

"Well I be! Abilene I'm so happy fer you" I shed a tear in my best friend's arms.

"Congratulations Abilence" a soft voice spoke behind, sendin' shivers up my spine.

"Thank you, Colton" she smiled. "Soon it'll be your turn, don't ya think, Millie?".

I hit her in the arm and she played innocent, askin' me why I did that. I was grateful fer the warm fire, usin' that as my excuse why my cheeks were turnin' red. Colton hopped up, followed by Brooks. I listened to them, until they drowned out and it was just me and the stars.

I honestly didn't know what was gonna happen to me now that I was done with school. Mama wanted me to get into college, but I didn't want to go fer more school, especially not knowin' what I wanted to do with my life.

Colton and Brooks got accepted into the police force, they were done with academy I guess. They weren't gonna be startin' out as top guns, but they had to start somewhere. I guess Hunter graduated with them too, so they'd be seein' each other a lot more.

I felt indifferent about it, didn't have much to go off from there. Brooks said Abilene would never have to work anymore, and I laughed cause I knew she had never worked a day in her life. We all laughed and I don't know why, but that got me comin' back to my senses.

I was leanin' on Colton, his arm wrapped 'round me with Brooks and Abe just across from us. Somehow we were already talkin' about somethin' new, like how the police never stop these parties.

"Do they know we come out here every year?" Abilene asked.

"Prolly not, wouldn't they stop them if they did?" I added

"Nah, they know" Brooks smiled. "They just don't care".

"No one ever gets hurt, goes missin', or ends up dead" Colton said. "It's under their radar since they did the same thing too when they were younger".

I dunno if that made me feel better of worse about the liquor I was drinkin'. I felt more at ease knowin' I wasn't gonna get caught, but I didn't like the idea of havin' no rules since there ain't anyone to enforce em'.

Brooks and Abilene ended up goin' to find someplace *quiet* after an hour or so. I guess they wanted to celebrate their engagement in private. I was left with Colton, which wasn't bad and I ain't never gonna complain about that.

"What did you wanna tell me?" I looked up at him, still restin' my head on his shoulder, more his chest now.

"How'd you know there was somethin' I had ta say?" he spoke like the people in this town.

"Too much to drink?" I teased.

"Never" his rosy cheeks burned red.

He readjusted our bodies so I was lookin' at him face on, still sittin' in his lap stayin' warm as the night chilled.

"I've got words fer you" his body inched closer.

"What is it?" I whispered. "I haven't got all night, Colton Norwood".

I was definitely under the spell of free will and straight up alcohol negligence, cause I knew I woulda never said them words aloud if not fer drinkin' them all night long. I knew he was too, cause he was actin' different, more careful.

He stared at me like a deer caught in the headlights before it runs away or gets hit by the truck. He didn't do nothin' different, but I felt everythin' shift. I was no longer a high school student, he was no longer a teenager. We were both grown and we knew what we wanted.

"I love you, Millie Maye" he said and I froze. "You don't gotta say anythin' right now either".

Maybe it was the liquid courage I'd been drinkin' all night, maybe it was just me bein' dumb and his words invitin' me in. I let him grab my face with his gentle hands and bring my face close to his.

"I'm going to work really hard to get us out of this town" he kissed my forehead, then my nose, even looked up at my eyes before takin' in my lips.

I panicked but told myself I was okay, that I wanted it. Soon enough, I calmed down and my hands grabbed his arms, adventurin' over the strong farmin' muscles and then his shoulders. He pulled back, but I reeled him in like I was some fishin' champion.

He tasted like sweet tea and pecan pie on my lips and I wanted more. I could've sworn I was high on warm honey from the sweet taste of his lips, and I didn't know what to do. It was like I had broken through a barrier, ran a mile, completed a race I had never stopped runnin' from until now.

I didn't care about the voices, faces, the terrible terrible things them men had done to me. I didn't care about nothin' at all because whatever I was feelin' now was far better than anythin'. I was safe, and I knew it entirely. Things were gonna be different now.

We finally pulled away from each other and he kissed my forehead before bringin' me in fer a hug. I could barely think straight as fireworks exploded in my belly and chimes cleared my thoughts and the persistent headache I never knew I had.

I wanted to tell Abe, I had to tell her right then and there of what just happened. I excused myself from Colton, tellin' him I had to use the bathroom. He offered to follow me since it was really just a "walk as far as you can in the woods so no one sees you and pop a squat". I told him no, kissin' him one last time, tellin' him I'd be back soon.

"Hurry" he smiled. "I'll be waiting for you".

I walked off towards where I thought Abe and Brooks would be, knowin' they'd be sane when I arrived. I couldn't stop smilin', my lips were warm when I touched em', my body was warm thinkin' about him.

They way he talked more like us when he was drunk. We all knew he was tryin' hard to cover up our local slang so he'd appear more educated, but we never said anythin' to him 'bout it. I laughed to myself like a lunatic in the woods, walkin' to only God knows where.

"What's so funny?" a harsh voice spoke.

My body froze, I knew him, I knew his voice. I was alone, *drunk*, I was alone. I brought my hands away from my lips and I told the man to go away. He only stepped on twigs, tellin' me without words he was comin' closer.

I told myself to move, to do somethin', but I couldn't. Cause in that moment, I knew I ain't never made anythin' up in my life, that everythin' did happen to me. That it wasn't gonna stop.

"Yer a sweet sinner" Hunter caressed my shoulders.

"What do you mean?" I could hardly breathe, my entire body soberin' up in a second.

"I saw ya with that boy, Millie" he squeezed me hard and didn't let go when I screamed.

He placed his hands over my mouth, a bit my nose too, and I couldn't breathe properly. I started panickin', didn't know what to do cause he was too strong.

"Ya can't be with him, ya know" he bent close to whisper in my ear. "Yer mine".

My eyes burst wide and I elbowed him in the stomach. He let go to entertain me and I fell to the ground, not before gettin' back up and runnin' towards where I came. I screamed fer someone to help, but I knew their music was too loud. I was far away, and no one knew I had even left.

Hunter grabbed onto my hair, pullin' me down and my head hit a rock. I cupped the back of my head knowin' I was bleedin', and I tried to stand.

My body went cold, like a corpse before it dies. He got on top of me, pinnin' my arms at my sides and he told me he wasn't gonna hurt me.

It's just that, I was his bird. The small and fragile bird he didn't know how to care fer, and so he did hurt me. He covered my mouth when I screamed and cried. He punched me in the face, lifted my head and slammed it down.

I could only look at the stars, his dark silhouette, and I felt tears from his eyes fall on my face that were quickly turnin' cold. He kept sayin' he was sorry, that he didn't want to hurt me. I cried with him, even told him it was okay.

Cause part of me knew I deserved it. Part of me knew life was too right in that moment and I ain't good enough fer it. I was only gettin' what I deserved.

I didn't know if he kept punchin' me, I lost feelin' in my face, even think he broke my ankle so I couldn't run. I felt nothin' except a painfully crisp cold overcome me. Sometimes I'd like to think I felt blood oozin' from the back of my head, mixin' with the dirt.

I was dyin' and I ain't never been more right in my entire life. Soon, the stars disappeared, and Hunter wasn't on top of me. I had no body, no vessel to hold in my soul, and I floated towards the heavens.

Towards hell.

I said goodbye to the life I lived as someone called *Millie Maye*. It was the name of who I was before Satan found me and recreated me entirely in his image alone.

CHAPTER VI

My ankles were itchin', they were burnin' to the bones. Everythin' was dark, like my eyes had been gouged out by somethin'. There was a stingin' pain so deep in my head I didn't know if I was actually alive.

I couldn't remember much of anythin'. I couldn't remember anythin' at all, except I was with Colton at the party. What did I do? I walked off cause he kissed me and I knew where Abe was and I had to tell her and I walked off and I left Colton and I walked off into the woods and I walked off and I was alone and I didn't hear anyone comin' fer me and I couldn't stop it.

And I died.

My body shot up like a bullet hissin' from its barrel when I finally came to my senses. I was breathin' too heavy, too sporadic, I was gonna pass out if I didn't calm myself. But I didn't care, and I didn't want to care.

The more I moved, the louder clankin' metal became and I realized it was my fault. My ankles were no longer on fire, they were engulfed by scorchin' flames. I tried releasin' the pressure, but my hands couldn't reach em', they were tied down with two feet of freedom's reign.

Even kickin' them wouldn't work cause they were bolted tight to the floor. I tried rememberin' how I got there, how I managed to chain myself up; feet and hands.

I was breathin' too loud, screamin' too loud, the chains on my ankles were too loud, the creak from the bed I laid in was too loud. I was too much. Footsteps came apparent as they quickly moved up a set of stairs near the closed door.

My body jolted itself straight and I fell on my back, against the firm mattress that was damp from my sweat. Keys clanked behind the door and my lips fumbled with a silent cry. My lower lip shook uncontrollably and I blinked my eyes hopin' they'd show me a different view.

I pretended I was asleep when they walked into the room, when they closed the door and the lock kissed itself hello. I was asleep, they couldn't hurt me if I couldn't remember. I was awake, I couldn't pretend to imagine it all in my head.

"Shh" he spoke in a low tone. "Yer home now".

I was shakin' and I couldn't control it, whimperin' too. His large hands caressed my sweaty head and I wanted to open my eyes so badly just to see his face, but even then I knew I couldn't see and it woulda been better not to.

"Ya don't have to be afraid of me anymore, June. I saved ya life".

He spoke. He said. He promised. He lied.

Hunter spoke. Hunter said. Hunter promised. Hunter lied.

His voice shattered bones in my body, drowned out my lungs, carried me to a fire I knew I'd burn in forever. He leaned in close, pressed a kiss to my lips and I bit him. I dunno what stupidity overcame me, but it was primal.

Blood dripped on my lips and I heard him laughin' to himself like I was barkin' up the wrong tree, that I did somethin' wrong. I even lowered my head, felt a little guilty fer it. I was messed up in the head.

He sat at the edge of my bed, near my waist, and told me not to move. His fingertips softly touched my ribs, then circled the lower part of my stomach, and it dipped. He smiled and his warm breath stayed over me while he kissed my hipbones. I raised my arms as far as they could, sittin' up my entire bein' and I went ape on him.

I hit his face and he laughed. I punched his stomach and he laughed. I shoulda joined fer how pathetic I looked in his eyes. He grabbed onto my arms and pinned them above my head before sittin' ontop of me. God I was glad I couldn't see him or the smile I knew was on his lips.

"Ya don't wanna be deader than a doornail, do ya love?" he whispered in my ear.

I whimpered, mouthed the word 'no' with little air. He said he understood how I was feelin', that I'd come around to him sooner than later. Said I had no choice but to love him back.

I remembered tryin' to push him off me, but I was too weak. I remembered tryin' to scream but my mouth was closed tight. I remembered him puttin' a needle in my neck and my body gettin' cold. The last thing my thoughts made up was him takin' off my clothes, takin' me like I was some ragdoll.

***

My eyes weren't swollen anymore, maybe they were. I could open and close them, see clear as day where I was. Half of me was grateful, other half didn't want my sight anymore. My head pounded, mouth was dry, body completely numb.

I was already cryin' silent by the time I came back into my body. I wasn't havin' a nightmare I could wake up from, I was livin' a reality I could die from. I knew I had to act crazy, act like I liked it. I knew I had to pretend to be his doll, do what he wanted.

I sat up, my bruised wrists were already unchained from last night. My eyes fell to my ankles that were wrapped in white bandages under the cuffs. The right one was in a cast made from black fabric. I was an animal fer smilin', but it was the first proof I had to begin the puzzle.

The smell of lavender distracted me, I couldn't see where it was comin' from cause it was me. My skin was washed, cleaned, and dried all durin' a time I couldn't remember. I was wearin' a long baby pink dress with spaghetti straps, somethin' I'd never choose fer myself.

Even my hair was washed and brushed at my side, exactly how he knew I liked it. Prolly because he enjoyed it like that too, said it covered more of me so others couldn't see what I was hidin' from the world.

My room was small with wooden floors and dark blue walls. The only light I had was from the one atop, and the small crack of light from the window. It stood ceiling to floor, but was only about three inches wide, couldn't be bothered to open also.

There was nothin' else besides my large bed that was tucked away in the corner, across from the door. I had no drawers or dressers, nothin' to change myself in. There was a door not too far away from the foot of my bed and I wondered what it was.

Wind howled outside like it was askin' me where I was. I whispered I was trapped, that I was stuck in the home of my childhood friend. That's what I was supposed to call him, since he let me loose every time. I think that's why part of me wasn't entirely flustered.

Hunter usually let me go.

When I was twelve, he trapped me in his parent's storm bunker for six hours. He brought me food, even played a game with me fer an hour or less before leavin'. He said he wanted to keep me there forever, that I wasn't ever goin' to leave.

He eventually let me go and mama was real mad when I finally got home. I told her I was stuck playin' a game with Hunter and she didn't care, said I scared the soul outta her. I assumed she'd have her panties in a twist over this one too.

I knew Hunter, and I knew his games, I just had to act like I was okay with what he was doin' and I'd be fine. He was already takin' care of me; like with the ankle he broke. It was all wrapped up and hurt a heck of a lot less too.

I thought I heard the floor creak by the door and when my eyes finally ventured there, I knew I wasn't hallucinatin'. I saw the shadow of two feet from behind the door, knowin' he was waitin' fer me to settle down before comin' in.

"Hello?" I whispered, tryin' to keep my voice steady.

He didn't say anythin', he didn't do nothin' to confirm it was him by the door. Unless it wasn't him and I really was in trouble. But I swore it was him last night, I swore it was him on top of me and not anyone else.

"Hunter?" I asked again. "You're scarin' me".

That time I wasn't pretendin'. That time I wondered what in the crackhead's basement was I doin', actin' like everythin' was okay. This time wasn't the same as them other times, this time was worse. I was horse shit and he the fly.

He never did them things to me like he did last night and the days before that. I didn't even know where I was. Didn't know who he became. I didn't know nothin' about anythin' besides I was a complete idiot fer thinkin' I was gonna live.

"Did ya look outside?" he whispered. "I made sure to give ya the best view".

I looked away though I knew he'd already seen my face. I sure as shit knew he'd find pleasure in my pains, it's not like he hadn't shown those high tendencies before.

He brought a tray in one hand and a small table in the other, settin' it down close to the bed I would soon rot in.

"I made ya tea" his breath was warm on my neck. "Drink it, will ya?".

I told myself to be still, but I was too stubborn to listen to myself. I turned in the bed, layin' on my side and I wished I hadn't. He grabbed my face in his hands and placed a forced kiss to my lips.

I dunno what overcame me, maybe it was the chains around my feet or the insensitive emotions I couldn't fester.

I slapped his face as hard as I could and he simply dropped his head near mine. I sat up and the chains tetherin' me clanked against the bed's legs.

He didn't say nothin' when he bent over my body, face to face. My breathin' was so loud, I couldn't hear nothin' over it. Hunter pinched his lips into a flat line and I winced when he grabbed onto my ankles. A silent scream escaped my lips and he told me to stay still, to be quiet, that he wasn't gonna hurt me.

"Why are you doin' this?" I placed a hand on my ankle, over his.

"Doin' what?" he kissed my hand and I managed to stand.

I stumbled on my toes and he acted like some divine savior, helpin' me stand on both my feet. My entire body was sore, standin' only made it worse. I couldn't do nothin' but fall to the ground. He cussed under his breath and pulled me up.

"That's my fault" he smirked.

I was gonna ask him what he meant like the idiot I was, but last night flooded in my head and drowned me out like a dam's walls breakin' fer the very first time without warnin'. *This town, this mind, didn't have enough time to escape.*

"Get off me" I whispered into a scream. "Get off me".

"Shh, it's okay. I won't hurt ya no more, I promise" he laced my arm over his shoulder so my weak and tortured legs could stand.

I ignored the persistent throbbin' in my inner thighs, arms, and ankle and I ran fer the door. Chains tugged on my legs and I fell before I could reach 'em. *I'm trapped.* If I thought I was panickin' before, there I was doin' it again.

"Come with me" he offered me his hand and I was foolish to think he was lettin' me out.

Hunter scooped me up with his cold and clammy hands, walkin' me to the small cutout of a window; I took note how far the chains let me travel. I tried pushin' away from him when his hand slid from my shoulder to my waist, then to the bottom of my butt.

"I promise you, my love. I won't-".

"Love?" I asked disgustingly, pushin' away from his body and failin', only makin' his grip tighter. "Hunter, you don't love me. You don't even know me".

"I know ya more than ya think ya do, June. You'll see soon enough that everythin' I ever done was fer ya".

He had the wrong person, he must've. My name wasn't June, wasn't even close. I was a Millie Maye, dumb enough to walk off into the woods to tell my best friend a secret I had no intentions of keepin'.

He said June like I was whoever he thought I was. Each sentence, every endin', he made it a point to speak them four letters to me. Said he was buildin' this home fer me since last year, tryin' to get me thinkin' there's no way out.

"Stop callin' me June, Hunter. You know my name" I kept pickin' at the scabbed prints on my hands.

"Stop callin' ya June?" he laced his fingers in mine, squeezin' so tight I thought one would pop right off. "Are ya feelin' okay, my love?".

I smacked his hand as he brought it to my forehead, tryin' to check my temperature like I was some insane bein'. I wasn't insane, was I? I wasn't experiencin' some type of memory loss? I smacked both sides of my head before I wasn't even allowed to do that and he held me like I was the abuser.

"What are yo-".

"Yer mine" his words dominated mine, pushin' me away towards the sliver of a window.

I pressed my forehead against the small thickness of the glass and the cat I never saw, that no one ever could see, caught my tongue like a drunken mouse and ran away with it before I could follow. *Corn.* There were corn fields everywhere.

His house, the prison he built fer me, the prison he'd kill me in was surrounded by corn fields. It wasn't surrounded by them and separated by roads or anythin' shoutin' at me fer escapes. It was in the dead middle.

The sound of his heavy feet slammed one by one as they cautiously approached me. Each thump recalibratin' the rhythms of my heart to sabotage the rest of my body. He whispered in my ear sayin' he wanted us to start over from the day we were kids.

He said I wasn't ready when we were younger, but I was now. I kept askin' what he meant, but he wouldn't listen, just kept sayin' there was time now fer him to do what he wanted. He was goin' to lock me in the room forever, and I had no way of escapin'.

I backed away and he followed, stupid I was fer thinkin' the room I had could've been mine with my own rules.

My eyes widened as his pinned. He never changed my name, he never did this to me like how he was doin' it now. This was different, *this is different*. I am goin' to die I said to him with the quiet voice I had.

"Ya became mine in June, so I'll call ya June" his hands wrapped 'round my throat and I squirmed "The harder ya push, the more painful this whole transition will be fer ya, June".

"I can't breathe" I clawed at them hands 'round my neck until he finally let go and pinned me to the wall.

He told me he'd been preparin' fer me, that everythin' he did was fer me and there ain't no turnin' round now. My mind played back the last few months and I remembered.

He left durin' school a lot and no one knew why, they even started askin' questions. When they did, he'd show up. Tried tellin' 'em he was overworked, but I didn't buy it. I knew, and now, I was in it.

I was gonna be sick and he knew it. He quickly grabbed the waste bin by the door and held it up at the perfect moment fer my stomach acid to say hi. I fell to the floor guided by his arms and I couldn't control myself as everythin' I had came up outta me.

"I think I gave ya too much" he whispered, movin' the hair from my face. "Don't worry, June. Soon we'll get married, have some babies, we'll build a life together. And if sometime later ya don't wanna live here no more, we'll leave".

I looked up at him fer the first time and saw the Devil's presence in his eyes. Hunter wasn't home no more, and I was gonna have to live with him fer as long as he wanted, until the day came when he wouldn't want me no more.

"What did you do to me?" I cried between chuckin' up stomach.

"Try to get some sleep, love" he kissed the top of my forehead. "Through that door is yer bathroom, it's just a toilet and sink. When yer ready I'll move ya into our room where you'll have yer bath".

I didn't bother rotatin' my head to know he was talkin' bout the door near my bed. I guessed the chains I was gonna have to get used to wearin' let me go there.

He stood up and the room suddenly got colder, shakin' me from the inside out. He told me to drink the tea he made, that'd it'd help with the headaches I was havin'. He also said to wash up the best I could cause he'd be back fer dinner.

I waited fer the door to crack shut, listened fer the lock to click, and counted only two steps before I couldn't hear him no more. Then, I lost it, cause I couldn't keep nothin' in. I grabbed onto that small metal waste bin like it was the messiah, and I cried fer everythin' I knew I'd lost.

He wasn't gonna let me go this time 'round. I knew I wasn't gonna have to make nothin' up explainin' where I was to mama and what I was doin' with whoever. Cause he was never gonna let me go.

And I would never need an excuse.

Cause I wasn't me anymore.

And I wasn't allowed to be.

CHAPTER VII

"Stay tuned to hear county sheriff, Gary Hinderston, give an update on Millie Maye".

I woke in a strange room, different than the one deemed my room until I was sane. It was dark, lit by only a few lights that made it hard to see 'round. There was a small coffee table in front of me, and a tv playin' past that, both of which were far away.

I watched smoke from the teacup float into the air, blurrin' out the tv's pictures and sound off in the distance. I was delusional watchin' it, but I somehow knew I'd have to find fun in the small things as such.

There were some heavy red curtains on the brown walls 'round, and I hoped there'd be some windows behind em'. Anythin' I could use to see daylight to count my days. I think I was layin' on a couch, but it was hard to tell cause my vision and bodily feelin' was only just now comin' back to me.

There was someone strokin' my hair, left me playin' opossum in his wake. *Hunter.* I shot up and crawled away to the corner of the couch, grabbin' onto my head I thought was gonna explode. I prayed to the lord, askin' him to save me, and if not, then take away the pain in my head.

"Shh, it's okay. I didn't want to wake ya" he reached fer me, placin' a warm hand on my shoulder.

He wore red flannel pajama bottoms and a grey t-shirt with a small hole near the right collar. I was in new clothes too, a light purple dress that stopped just below my knees, and thin straps holdin' everythin' up.

"How did I get here?" my hands fell over the thin cloth of my gown. "I don't remember comin' down".

Hunter's eyes bugged for a split second before smilin', like he was shocked at what I had to say that wasn't only varmint. He told me I was in the livin' room, carried me down cause I was sleepin' when he went up to get me.

I traced the bruises left on my wrists and he grabbed onto them, placin' a wet kiss on each hand. I pulled away, but he wouldn't let me. Somethin' in his eyes changed, they were like them animals I seen in school documentaries just before they were gonna do somethin' sinful.

I stood, too quickly, and I fell right back where I was planted. My ankles ached, burned even. I thought I could smell the iron in my blood on 'em if I tried hard enough. I found their post, I was anchored near the couch, and there was another spot fer me a few feet away.

I was like a dog on a fixed leash that people kept outside. Sometimes they move the steak for em', just so they can run 'round somewhere new. I was like that dog, only fer me, I didn't understand why.

"It hurts" I pointed to the cuffs. "Can ya take em' off?".

He ran a hand around my ankles, even brought up one of my legs to kiss where it hurt. He dropped my leg back to the floor before whisperin' he didn't trust me, that I'd have to show him I could be trusted fer him to let me go.

I had to be good, I had to be kind. I kept tellin' myself to make him happy so he'd give me freedoms, then I could leave. Only then, maybe I could escape with my life. His hand slid up my leg and under my dress before I knew what he was doin'.

I pushed him away when he grabbed onto my underwear and I heard it tear. He smiled like he knew what he was doin' was one of God's deadly sins, but he didn't care. His hands and fingers explored more than I screamed fer him not to, and he let go.

Just like that; I screamed and he stopped. He looked at me like he wasn't finished, but he would end it fer now. Jesus save me cause I didn't know how much longer I could live like that.

"Ya ain't eat yet, let me fix ya up somethin' good. I made steak and potatoes, but if ya want somethin' else, I'll get it" Hunter stood and my eyes followed.

The kitchen was right behind the livin' room, open concept where you could watch tv while cookin' at the stove. There was a small, uncovered, window above the sink on the opposite wall. It was dark out already, my body was painfully tired, yet I didn't do nothin' all day.

He opened the fridge door and the light made me turn away, but not quick enough fer me to see more posts in the floor that I could be connected to. He looked at somethin' near the bottom fer a while before grabbin' somethin' from the top shelf, closin' the door.

"And the clothes?" I hesitated to ask, mainly cause I didn't wanna hear he changed me again. "Did I put 'em on?".

He didn't answer, didn't say nothin'. He put the food on a plate and threw it in the microwave. I stared and watched the entire time to make sure he didn't put nothin' in it. Not that I was gonna eat it, I was starvin', but not hungry enough to eat his food.

When the ol' box finished, he popped out the food and brought it over to me, told me to be careful. I told him I wasn't hungry and he pinched his lips, furrowed his brows, and I knew I messed up.

"Ya don't like yer room, yer clothes, and now ya don't like yer food?" he laughed. "I'm startin' to think ya just don't like me".

He threw the plate onto the coffee table and my eyes followed to the tv. I sat up, starin' at my high school yearbook picture on its screen. My jaw dropped and I pointed like a little kid lookin' at somethin' weird fer the first time in its life.

"They're havin' a hard time findin' ya, June" he smiled, turnin' on the sound. "We all are".

I pulled my knees to my chest, coverin' myself with a blanket I found behind me. I couldn't do nothin' but watch the report about myself like it was some sort of sick game of Hunter's he wanted me to play in.

"An update on the recent high school graduate, Millie Maye" an older woman spoke. "This missing person case has hit another end as investigators are struggling to find any leads pertaining to her disappearance".

"We've been workin' around the clock fer the past two weeks tryin' to figure out somethin', anythin' leadin' us to her" Gary Hinderston wiped his brow.

Fer the past two weeks. I blinked my eyes and looked 'round the house like a zombie woulda wakin' up fer the first time. I only had memory of two nights, not two weeks. *He's druggin' me.* I looked back at Sheriff Hinderston.

He was an older gentlemen, large and round, baldin' brown hair and a large caterpillar mustache coverin' part of his top lip. I had no faith in him findin' me. Bless his heart even if he did, there ain't no way he'd outrun Hunter.

"This is a tricky case" he said again. "Them kids told us everythin' they knew, and still, we don't have much. Millie didn't tell no one where she was goin' after leavin' the party, she left no traces, even her cell and wallet were left behind".

But I'm here. I'm right here. My eyes hardened and I swore to myself under my skin fer not tryin' hard enough to escape Hunter that night, fer not screaming loud enough, fer not fightin' as much as I coulda.

"My poor baby" my mama's voice called me back.

She looked a mess. Her dark hair was disheveled and flew in the wind untamed. She was lookin' smaller too, I could tell she wasn't eatin' like she shoulda. I silently told her to stay strong and have faith that I was alive.

"I just want answers" she cried. "My Millie Maye is a good girl; she wouldn't ever do nothin' to put herself in harms way. Please, if you know anythin', come clean. I just want my baby girl home".

She could hardly speak; she was breakin' apart more than I ever saw her. Even when daddy left, she never cried that hard. My tears were fallin' fast and hard too, I couldn't control them like I wanted to. I didn't want Hunter to see me weak like he thought I was.

"I love you, Millie. Please come home" Abilene was next.

She talked about our relationship, that I was a good person and wouldn't hurt no one. She told them cameras I just wanted a normal life and how she blamed herself fer my disappearance. Said she shoulda been with me the entire time, how she wasn't supposed to leave me.

Mama pulled Abilene away and I watched them sit and cry in the corner of the camera's panel before they were like me and left completely.

"I will find whoever did this, and-".

Hunter turned off the tv, leavin' us in a dark room. I knew why he did it. He didn't want me to see who was talkin', but just a second of their soft and deep voice and it was too late. It was Colton, promisin' to avenge me if anythin' were to happen to a single hair on my head.

Hunter didn't want me gettin' hope from someone who ain't him.

"It's too bad we couldn't watch my part" I felt him lean closer. "I gave a pretty compellin' speech about not givin' up, that yer still alive, and whoever took ya better watch out fer me and God".

"Let me hear it" I asked, hopin' I could hear the end of Colton's speech.

"I'm a lot of things, but stupid ain't one, June" he laughed. "That boy was takin' advantage of ya when I saw y'all kissin' at that party. I know ya just wanna hear his voice one last time".

"You were watchin' me?" I cried.

"I had to! Ya can't be so easily trusted, especially with that guy. He's the worst thing fer ya and I woulda been dumber than flies on shit to let him keep touchin' ya like that. In fact, I'm still tryin' to decide what I wanna do with him".

There ain't nothin' you can do fer him to ever give up. Hunter got even closer, takin' away the blanket. I put my legs back down, squeezin' my thighs and hopin' the chains were louder than they actually were so he'd take it as a warnin'.

"Listen, June, I-".

"You're deranged" I spit at him.

"No" he grabbed onto my jaw, squeezin' tightly to hold me in place. "I'm in love".

"You wouldn't know what love was if it hit you upside the head! You're hurtin' me" I cried.

"I don't care" he tossed my head like a sack of stones and I fell off the couch. "Ya better learn to not piss me off real quick".

I hit my head on the coffee table and I could hardly look up. I grabbed onto the sides of my pulsatin' head and blinked my eyes fer my vision to return normal. Loud pains shot behind my head and into my neck, I think the back of my head never healed and was bleedin' again.

"Hunter, stop, please" I lifted a hand to keep him away. "My heads hurtin' real bad, please".

He was screamin' at me and callin' me disrespectful fer everythin' I ever did to him. Was tellin' me I owed him my life fer havin' him save me, that he was gonna give me the best life I coulda imagined and I needed to start bein' grateful fer it.

I asked him to stop, screamed back at him to take me home. My heart was beatin' so fast, my dress was lifted past my thighs, and I couldn't stop cryin'. He made his way fer me and my vision got spotty again.

I was hyperventilatin' like I was gonna get a lickin' worthy of death when he came closer. He sprawled between my thighs and I couldn't even kick him away because the chains were pulled tight, my runnin' round length was all used up.

He pushed my shoulders to the ground. I felt him between me, and he kissed my lips and I bit hard on 'em like I'd been missin' fer two weeks and not two days. He pushed off me, grabbin' onto his bloody lip and cussed like a sailor.

"Ya done it now, June" he raised his fist before I could question.

He got on top of me, pinnin' my arms at my sides like we were in the woods again. One fist after the other, I heard my nose crack and my jaw snap wide. There was so much unbearable pain, I couldn't feel none of it.

My head fell to the windows lookin' out, showin' me nothin' but corn stacked on corn fer miles. I wondered if I were still in Louisianna, still in the small town I was startin' to hate. He put his hands 'round my throat, tryin' to get me to look at him, but I didn't want to. There was a red balloon flyin' by and gettin' caught in one of the stalks.

I wasn't in my body again, I was lookin' through my memories, wonderin' if there were one I could jump into and hide in. I screamed when I pulled out one I ain't have no memory of makin', one from the night before or the hours from earlier.

> *I was still awake when I heard hunter comin' up the stairs and openin' the door to my room. I was still sittin' in the corner, bucket of vomit wrapped in my arms like it were a baby, and tears frozen to the sides of my cheeks.*
>
> *I smelt, I was a mess, I was a captive prisoner fer the first time and it wasn't a joke. I had sat there all day not thinkin', not wonderin' why me. I had given him too many reasons to choose me. I ain't never spoke up about him, I went back to him after what he did to me.*
>
> *I was where I was cause it was my fault, and my fault entirely. There ain't anyone to blame but myself, cause I never told anyone. I wondered throughout the day what would happen if I told someone about everythin' he did to me.*
>
> *Would he have gotten into trouble with his mama or the police? Would they take his clean football record and call him a saint, and that I was just someone lookin' fer attention? I wondered if he would've been sent to prison and if Timothy woulda killed me that night.*

Hunter was at the door, I heard him fumblin' like he had butter on his hands while lookin' fer the right key. I wondered if every door in this insufferable house had a lock just fer me, because of me.

"June, I made dinner" he poked his head 'round the door.

I didn't say nothin', just sat there hopin' he'd leave since I wasn't goin' to eat his food anyway. He walked in after a few quick moments passed, sat at my side, and tucked hair behind my ears like I was a mess.

"Ya haven't moved" he breathed heavy near my face. "I told ya to clean up as best as ya could, didn't ya hear me?".

Again, I said nothin', just stared far in front of me, starin' at that sick cornfield I knew he'd built his home in just to get a rise outta me.

"Gimmie some sugar, huh?" he tried touchin' my shoulders, said I needed to get washed up.

I looked away from him, pissin' him off and he grunted loudly under his breath to make it known I done just that. He took off his dark blue flannel and tossed it onto the bed he called my temporary one.

"I've tried to be patient, but I ain't got any, so it's kinda hard, June" he said I wasn't makin' an effort.

Hunter grabbed onto my face and placed a hot kiss on my forehead before I threw the waste bin at him. He backed away to examine my stomach's food and acid on his nice clothes. Then, somethin' changed, somethin' clicked in his head that I couldn't understand.

And I knew too late, all too well, that I messed everythin' up.

He pulled the chains controllin' my ankles, pullin' me closer to him feet first. I couldn't squirm away from him cause he dragged me into a corner. He got on his knees, liftin' up my thin dress, and unzipped his pants before I could scream. I tried tossin' 'round, but it only made things easier fer him.

He flipped me over on my belly and held me down by the inner parts of my thighs, havin' his way with me like he wanted. I couldn't even cry, I couldn't even breathe. His skin was diggin' into mine, and mine was diggin' into the wooden floors.

He tore the back of my dress off, just to place filthy kisses on my back. Just to whisper to my body that he would buy me another in any color I wanted.

I laid there still, not feelin' my body rock harder into the ground, not feelin' my nails break as they scratched deep into the floor, not feelin' my hipbones bruise deeply against the ground.

I couldn't remember when he finished, my brain was a wasteland swamp, filled with hot springs that hid these kinds of memories from curious hands, my own hands as a matter of fact.

He was bathin' me in hot water that smelt of lavender soap. He even dressed me in a light purple dress with thin straps, a promise he made earlier. My eyes stayed closed the entire time, my skin felt numb the entire time.

My body was his, never to be mine again, and even then, I wouldn't want it back.

CHAPTER VIII

I played his game like he wanted, still, it wasn't worth it. No matter the things I did fer him, I did 'em wrong. I did every single thing wrong in them eyes of his and I ain't got nothin' but bruises and broken skin to show fer it.

"Ready?" he popped his head inside my room.

I looked 'round the once bare room that was now filled with a full dresser of things he wanted to see me in, bedsheets that made nighttime a little less painful, and paintings hung on the walls. Hunter said he was happy fer the way I'd been actin'.

It was all a mask though, I was just tryin' to get on his good side, hopin' he'd leave one day fer work like he always did and forget to chain me up. I dunno how long it's been since I was last takin', days seemed to go by quickly while the nights teased me they could go slower than the previous, and they did.

He stopped chainin' me up at night, but the bedroom door was secured by a serious amount of locks. Even if I wanted to, I ain't have the means to get outta there. Tried it one time and he chained me back up fer maybe a week or half.

All I did was wait by the door with one of them dresser drawers in hand. I waited fer hours in the night, lookin' through the small peep hole I had to call a window. He finally came up from a drunken night with his friends, he was sloppy.

Just that once I wanted him to feel my pleasure, and so, I snapped. He walked through the door and I slammed the dresser on his head. He thumped to the ground and swore at me. I ran out, jumpin' over his body that laid across the border to freedom.

God I was so close, but he was faster. He grapped onto my left ankle and slammed me down, swearin' at me to stop movin', sayin' I was flyin' off the handle. I kicked and scratched, turnin' over to see his boilin' red face. He said he didn't want to hurt me, but I couldn't stop cryin'.

Cause he did just that, hurtin' me in ways I wished he could feel. Again, and again, till he got his fill and left me on the cold floor while I looked up at the ceiling wonderin' 'why me?'. I got over it though, suppressed it down knowin' no amount of therapy could help me if I ever made it out.

Sometimes I felt like I was in a game. Each mornin' was a new level, and if I failed, the dark night would bring its punisher. It was no surprise that I failed, each and every night, I was scared I didn't die.

I'd hoped he'd just forget about me fer one night, then I could try leavin'. He almost did.

He almost did.

> *I couldn't remember the time he'd come home, but he sure was loud about it. Heard the front door open fer the first time in my life before it slammed shut, takin' away all hopes I had. My eyes opened wide as I laid in my bed, tryin' to prepare for his pleasure and my pain.*
>
> *He called it an 'exchange' whenever he wanted my body. Told me I owed him 'this one little thing' in*

return fer the food, water, shower, and shelter. I told him I didn't want none of it and I pissed him off, makin' that night slow and painful.

His boots stumbled their way up the stairs and to the foot of my door. I tensed, I closed my eyes, I prayed to God to save me from this one night. I guess I didn't pray loud enough, cause he ain't never heard me before, there was no reason God was gonna listen to me now.

The door quietly creaked open and I closed my eyes, pretendin' to sleep. One night I did just that and he let me be, just rubbed my thighs and stomach fer a while before leavin'. God was I dumb thinkin' it'd work again.

I had no more chains at night, tried to use that against him and it was a mistake. He ended up fixin' that dresser so the drawers couldn't get out. Since then, I ain't have nothin' to use against him.

I tried doin' pushups, squats, stuff to make me seem bigger and bulkier, but he controlled my meals, and I ain't have enough food in me to feel strong enough to keep on doin' them. That was besides the point. I knew I needed to sharpen my mind before anythin' else.

He walked to my side and I opened my eyes, pretendin' like I was happy to see him. His drunk smile told me he wasn't there, he ain't even home, and my smile turned realer than a bull fightin' red.

"Let's go to bed, June" he picked me up and I let him. "I ain't gonna hurt ya tonight, I promise".

He ain't never talked to me so softly before, ain't never carried me like I was a baby bird in a child's arms. If he hadn't been so tied up in the beginnin', maybe then he'd have someone he ain't gotta pretend with.

His room was in the next one over, but mine didn't even look like the entrance to one. The door looked like a bookshelf, somethin' no one would question. That's why I could only hear close to nothin' from the inside.

He kicked open the door, kickin' it shut too like it was supposed to impress me. He placed me on the large bed across from the door, fixin' itself between dressers and another bathroom. It was clear as day which side was supposed to be mine.

He filled it with all them girly things he had me wearin', even had a place I could do my makeup at, even though I ain't never wore any. He locked the door with a bolt and put the key in the pocket of his flannel, givin' it a good tap.

"I'm gonna get washed up" he headed fer the bathroom on his side. "Don't try anythin' stupid".

He kept the door open as he turned on the large shower and stripped naked fer me to see. I looked away and turned towards the things that were supposed to be mine, hopin' I could find somethin' sharp.

I was gettin' used to livin' with him. I started forgettin' what mama looked like, was havin' troubles recallin' her voice, the same fer everyone. I knew I wasn't supposed to, but life was less uncomfortable because it was predictable.

I looked back at Hunter through the clear glass panels of the shower, who was already submerged in water. His head was pointed towards the tap with closed eyes and his hands rest on the shower's wall.

I looked through my dresser, hopin' to find somethin' different to sleep in. I was tired of them dresses he had me wearin' night and day. I found a pair of shorts that could've counted fer long underwear and I put em' on under the short dress.

"June" hunter called out and I asked why. "We ain't gonna be doin' any of that tonight, you ain't gotta worry".

I simply said okay and continued lookin' round fer a shirt or somethin'. All he had was tank tops and bralettes fer me. I sighed defeat and walked to his side, knowin' dang well he had his eyes fixed on me.

I opened his dresser drawers like a feral animal until I found where he kept his shirts. I tried not to act surprised after noticin' how clean he kept everythin'. I tossed on a dark shirt of his and smiled when it covered my shoulders and half of my arm.

Hunter was bigger than me, there was no doubt our height difference made for awkward conversation, but fer the first time, I was feelin' good about it. Cause it meant I was covered more than I ever had been since gettin' here some time ago.

With a towel wrapped around his waist, he walked outta the bathroom. I didn't act like I wasn't doin' anythin' I ain't supposed to. I closed the drawer and kept my hands of the wood frame as he pressed himself against my back.

"Ya don't like yer clothes?" he kissed the top of my head.

I didn't say nothin', just stood there in fear like an opossum playin' dead. His hands fell to my shoulders and he played with his shirt's fabric before turnin' me 'round to get a good look at me.

"I wanted to wear somethin' with more-" I was bold.

"Ya don't gotta explain" he smiled near my lips. "I think I actually prefer ya in my clothes".

His hands slid down my arms and to my waist and I shuddered with a cry in my throat. He said he wasn't gonna hurt me, but I don't think he knew what that meant. Our dictionaries didn't have the same vocabulary.

He twined his hand in mine and walked me to the bed, tellin' me which side was mine and which was his, followed by the words he didn't care, as long as I was happy. I didn't fight back, didn't kick, cry or scream, he wasn't doin' nothin' to me.

He lifted the sheets and waited fer me to crawl in before walkin' back to his dresser and putiin' on a pair of flannel pajamas. The key is in his shirt, and his shirt is in the bathroom. I turned away and let him wrap his warm body around mine when he came back.

He moved the large fabric away from my neck and kissed my skin before coverin' it back up again.

Somethin' about himself was different, like it were the real version of him. A piece I knew I'd have to hold onto if I weren't ever gonna make it out.

I waited fer minutes, maybe even an hour fer him to fall asleep, smellin' the alcohol on his breath penetrate the skin on the back of my neck. His grasp was gettin' softer too, tellin' me I was the only aware one in that house.

There were two large windows on both sides of the bed, lettin' in the moon's light and I used it to look round more. That room was designed fer me, fer us to live in together. Them other rooms I ain't never been in were fer the children he wanted to have, the family he wanted to create.

If I was never gonna make it out, then I was gonna have to uphold them standards of his. I was gonna have to let him do what he wanted with me, and I was gonna have to be okay with it. But I wasn't, cause this ain't a case of Stockholm syndrome.

I had mama who I ain't seen in weeks or months, Abilene I ain't talked to, Colton I ain't kissed, and a life I ain't yet lived. I waited longer fer his breathin' to fall heavy and his arms too. I squirmed, not even an inch, and he pulled me into him.

"Don't act hog wild on me" he whispered in my ear.

Hunter's heart was beatin' calm against my back, his thighs pressed tightly against the backs of mine. One arm outstretched under my head like a pillow, holdin' my hand with his, and the other was wrapped tight round my waist.

"I was turnin' towards ya" I whispered a lie.

He smiled against my cheek and helped me keep promise to my lie by turnin' me towards his face. His lips pressed against my forehead and then between my eyes before fallin' to my lips. I had to play his part, make him love me enough to let me go.

I swallowed the turnin' vomit in my throat back down and I kissed him fer the very first time. He told me I was temptin', but that he promised me already how he wasn't gonna try nothin'. He caressed my cheek with his thumb and then with his lips.

I tried not to cry, tried not thinkin' about Colton and wonderin' if he already forgot about me, if everyone already had. I tried not thinkin' about the drugs I was on, how my feet couldn't walk straight lines, how I couldn't remember the night before when I woke up with sore legs, a broken nose, fist, ankle, wrist, or more.

"Yer turnin' out to be a good girl" his lips last spoke before fallin' off to sleep.

I counted three hours before movin' on my own. I counted one hundred and eighty minutes, ten thousand and eight hundred seconds before quietly liftin' my body from the bed. I tiptoed on creakin' wood as I made way to the bathroom.

Hunter stirred in bed and I wanted to jump back in, cover my head with the sheets and beg for his forgiveness cause I knew he'd wake angry, but I didn't, cause he never did. I hurried to the laundry bin and grabbed the orange and blue flannel he teased me with.

"No" I whispered, bitin' down a cry.

There weren't any keys in the pocket, weren't nothin' I could use to get myself outta the room. I sat on the floor and leaned the bin on my legs, searchin' like a racoon lookin' fer treasure in the trash.

Piece after piece, there ain't nothin' I coulda found to put a smile on my lips. I was cryin', tears fallin' down my face like a waterfall smoothin' stone in a day.

"June?" Hunter's soft whisper stood me straight.

He was leanin' on the bathroom archway, starin' at me with humble eyes and a look that wasn't angry, surprised, or upset.

"Ya ain't gonna find them in there" he outstretched his hand fer me to take.

I had two options; act like I liked him, or run. I knew damn well runnin' wasn't gonna do anythin' fer me but piss him off. Runnin' was gonna make him angry, was gonna let him hurt me.

Act sane. Act like you like it. If I am to be selfish, let me be wisely selfish. I took his hand and had him help me up and take me back to bed. The sheets were still warm, almost like they were makin' fun of me fer never leavin'.

"Don't lay so far away" he pulled me in close, my back stern on his bare stomach.

It was strange knowin' my abuser loved me enough to steal me, rape me, torture me, endlessly make me feel like I was the psychotic traitor fer not returnin' his love. I sighed to myself, loud enough fer him to react, but he didn't stir.

"Will you ever let me go?" I whispered to the silent room.

Moments passed and he didn't say anythin' and I wondered if he were truly asleep, if I'd out beaten him in somethin' as childish as to see who would fall asleep first.

"I won't have to" he kissed my neck and then turned my head to kiss my lips as I laid numb.

So there I was, lookin' at him like I loved him as he walked into the room meant only fer me. The room he sent me to sleep in when he didn't want to look at me, or when his personality he never remembered came out to play games of horror and pain.

"Just a second" I walked to the dresser, slippin' on some thick socks.

Days were gettin' colder, trees were turnin' red, orange, and yellow. There were less things to cry out about at night. I only really remembered Mama and Abilene. I wasn't allowed to remember or think about Colton, it showed too much on my lips when Hunter placed empty kisses on me.

Got me in trouble one time too when I called out Colton's name when Hunter and I were sleepin' in the same bed. He told me it was a nightmare and that's why I was hollerin', that he hurt me and I had to forget about him.

I didn't correct Hunter even though he was wrong, I didn't think about doin' anythin' that'd make him feel like he was wrong. I knew it'd come back to bite me in the butt as a punch to the face, kick in the stomach, or an unwelcomed body between my legs.

"Ya know this hurts me more than it hurts ya" he locked a cuff on each of my ankles.

I smiled, gave him a nod, and kissed his cheek before followin' him down twelve steps, turnin' right after makin' a left, and stoppin' in the kitchen. He chained me up to the post in the middle of the room and told me to be careful with the knives.

My attention span really was like a child's glare. I was starin' straight at the knives in their holder to the right of the stove, questionin' it all. Hunter left me and walked into the open livin' room, not takin' his eyes off. He called out again that he'd love whatever it was I made.

I waved him off and kept my eyes fixed on the knives before drawin' out the biggest one. I thought about hurtin' myself, thought about stabbin' him or my chest, got real close to doin' it too. I held the blade in the runnin' sink, with my wrist firm against it.

I knew Hunter couldn't see what I was doin', especially when I told him I needed to wash everythin' before cookin'. He laughed back and told me I had OCD and I wanted to fling the blade between his eyes. I took a deep breath and pinned the blade deeper against myself.

I wanted to die, wanted him to clean up my blood and hide my body. I wanted his DNA all over me and fer the police to know exactly who did this to me. But God finally spoke with memories of Abe, mama, and Colton.

God finally said he was with me, that I was gonna be okay if I held on just a little while longer. My wrist began to bleed with a sharp pain and I smiled cause I was the one that did it. Even then, I knew that ain't the way. I was a woman of faith who wasn't gonna go against the Lord.

I dropped the knife into the sink and it clanked against the porcelain sides. Hunter shot up and ran to my side, takin' my wrist in his palm and runnin' a paper towel over it.

"Ya did this on purpose?" he yelled at me, jumpin' me from my skin.

I didn't want him to hurt me, didn't want him to use me, so I lied again and shook my head. I was simply gonna be the perfect person Hunter wanted me to be.

"No" I wrapped my arms around him. "I didn't mean to, it just slipped once I put the soap on it, I swear to God".

He held me tightly and kissed the top of my forehead, sayin' he loved me and talkin' about how delicate I was. He told me he'd make our dinner, but I insisted on doin' it fer us. I insisted on bein' the silent housewife with a secret only we knew.

I pulled away and he lifted my head with just a finger, placin' a kiss on my lips and I let him. I think I saw him smile, blush even, before walkin' towards the fridge with the knife in his hand.

"I'll do the chopin', you do the cookin', June".

I laughed at his jokes, took his hand to slow dance in the kitchen like he wanted, even kissed him without askin' fer him to think I was bein' a good girl. I'm pretty sure he saw right through it though, even the slow dancin' part.

Colton always told me we'd dance slow, take our time when he got us a place of our own. I pretended like I was dancin' with him. I pretended like it was his arms caressin' my shoulders, movin' his way to my lower back.

Hunter carried our dishes to the wooden framed dinin' room table, not far from the couch in the livin' room. He put some music on the tv, even lit a candle too. I sat facin' the kitchen, Hunter the tv. He grabbed my hands and bowed his head, sayin' a prayer to the Lord, God.

"Dear, Lord. We ask that you bless this food, home, and family. May we live through you in selfless servitude and humility. May we only attract positivity, love, and health. Dear God, I pray that June comes around to see all that I do fer her".

"I do" I wanted to vomit.

He was tryin' to mess with my head, I think he was.

"Amen" he slapped his hands and dug in.

I watched him eat quickly as I slowly took bites of my own food. It was good, real good, and I wasn't sure if he'd ever let me cook again after the knife incident. I choked down a tear as the breaded chicken made way down my throat, it was mama's recipe.

The closest way I could get to her, feel her with me, was through her cookin'. She rarely had the time with all them jobs, but when she did make somethin', they were masterpieces.

Hunter threw down his napkin, laid back in his chair, and told me to get some rest while he washed dishes. Since he already moved my chain limits to the one near the couch, he didn't have to exchange em' again fer me to lay down.

I sat on the soft couch; he tossed me the remote and told me I could put on whatever. Though I knew he'd look at what I was watchin' from afar, I just had to see if it were on. I headed straight fer channel two, hopin' to see mama, but I was forgotten.

They were already on their next news report, talkin' about some old lady who died in her home last night. I tossed the remote on the coffee table and laid on my back as the meaningless words of the news reporter silently washed through the house.

I stared at the ceilin', listenin' to Hunter scrub away at the oiled pans I knew would be hard to clean. If that breaded chicken meant anythin', it was a miserable clean up. If I were gonna have to live with him fer longer than I wanted, then I was gonna make it under table interestin'.

"This just in" the news reporter spoke loudly. "It seems the search for missing Millie Maye isn't over".

I shot up and searched fer the remote, tryin' to turn it down before Hunter could hear it.

"Leave it" he placed a hand on each of my shoulders.

"After a long and brutal wait for the laboratory to inspect the DNA sample found where Millie Maye may have gone missing, the results have come back positive".

"Shit" Hunter cussed under his tongue, not knowin' I heard it.

"This opens authority for more police, squads, and local help to search for Millie. Not only do police officers have more information about what happened that night, but they can also increase their funding to find the missing resident as the penalties have increased".

Hunter's grasp hardened, diggin' into the meat in my shoulders. I put my hands on his and rubbed my thumb over 'em. The tv showed a search party goin' through the woods, crime scene analysists tapin' off segments, and then a press conference with Mama and Abe.

They didn't say nothin', just sat exhausted, depleted, skinnier than bones wearin' thin flesh suits. I couldn't even cry for 'em, cause I knew if I did, Hunter was gonna hurt me fer it. The screen flashed again to a new scene; it was the inside of the police station.

"Shut it off!" Hunter yelled.

"This only confirms my suspicions" the new officer said with anger in his throat. "Everyone was ready to give up, said she ran away like most do once they graduate, but I knew her better. Millie was taken and I will not give up until I find the person responsible".

"Shut it off, June, or so help me God" he ran 'round the couch, divin' fer the remote on the small table.

Don't give up.

Colton.

Don't give up.

"If you're watchin' this, my Millie" mama spoke, cryin' between each vowel. "We're not givin' up. I can feel your heart beatin' and I know you ain't dead. Please, baby girl, keep fightin'- fer me".

The remote fell onto the hardwood floors and the batteries scattered across the ground. I couldn't do nothin' even if I wanted to. I was frozen in my chair when I saw a release of hundreds of red balloons scatter across the screen fer me.

They were fer me and I saw one once too. It was the first time he brought me down to the livin' room. It was the first time I saw outside from somethin' larger than a sliver in the wall. The balloons on the tv had strings with my picture and a visual description of who I was, the one I saw had nothin'.

I was still in my hometown.

I was still home.

I was only a few miles away from mama.

The screen died black and I looked up. Hunter unplugged the device from the wall like some deranged animal separatin' organs from a body fer fun. He walked towards me, stompin' his feet, raisin' his fist. There was a burr in his saddle and I knew it had already poked too hard.

"I told ya to shut it off" his fist came down hard, knockin' me off the couch. "Why didn't ya listen?".

"I'm sorry" I whispered.

He lifted up my head by my hair and spit on my face, callin' me disgustin'. I didn't say nothin', couldn't move if

I wanted to. My body went completely numb, abandonin' me from myself. He tossed me on my back and beat me until my skin was ice and my heart was barely beatin'.

My blood felt cold.

I wasn't gettin' out.

So maybe I should've stopped pretendin' like I was.

CHAPTER IX

It'd been a few days since I last seen Hunter. His knickers were in a knot cause I told him I was tired one night when he invited me to his room. It was a painful mistake on my part, especially the three days he never gave me food.

It was the first time he asked if it was what I wanted and I said no. He took it personal, as he should've. I wasn't goin' to forget everythin' he'd done and kept doin' to me. Yet again, I felt so defenseless, powerless, against him.

He beat me that night, told me I was again ungrateful fer everythin' he'd done fer me. Told me my mama was dead too, but apologized fer that hours later. I believed him though when he told me she wasn't doin' too good.

"Yer mama was lookin' real bad today, June" he cradled me in his arms.

We laid on the hardwood floor, my body completely numb yet aware of everythin' he had just done to me. Told me I was his pet when he finished, scooped up my naked body in his arms and held me to the floor as he fit himself behind.

"I wish ya could see her" he whispered to my head. "It'd help her a lot ya know. But I just can't trust ya enough to believe ya wouldn't try runnin' away from me, creatin' some type of story in yer head that ain't true".

I cried as I smelt mama on his skin. Hunter spent his whole day consolin' my mama and his. Said Colton was there, that he gave up quickly once they hit a dead end in my case.

Abe helped mama that day, I guess they were hostin' a farewell party fer me. Mama didn't want to have it, thought I was still alive, but it was the sheriff that encouraged it all. Seemed like my case was just like any other, only my endin' hadn't come yet.

There I was, sittin' on the shower floor as the hottest waters burned my skin too cold and not enough fer me to enjoy the pain. I was numb, alone, and so empty it was hard to even cry anymore. I knew what to expect most days.

I woke up to a small portion of breakfast waitin' fer me on the small table near the bed. I never heard Hunter walk among the creaky floors, never heard him place the tea and breakfast on the old table. I think he was back to druggin' me, it was the only thing that made sense.

Then I'd wait. I'd wait and wait fer him to come back with some news about his day at work, and his visit with his mama and mine. I'd listen to his voice and wished I could gouge out my ears or beg him to stop without repercussions.

When the sun fell and the moon rose, it was my turn to entertain him. I'd cook him dinner, most of the time he let me have free range, so I'd try to remember everythin' mama taught me. Those were the times I missed her most, when I failed to remember the things she said to my little head and I didn't listen.

I'd fall asleep on the couch, wake up in my room with new bruises I couldn't remember but could only assume where from. That's what I was doin' now, lookin' at my body with disgust cause it wasn't mine. Sometimes I wondered if I swapped with another.

Bite marks from "playtime" ran up and down my thighs and gashes penetrated my ankles from the tightenin' of the cuffs when I couldn't move so well. Against my own wants, I wasn't myself.

Just June.

I sighed and let the hot water burn my scalp as I looked down at the drain, coverin' it from time to time to splash my hands in the poolin' waters.

"June?" his voice called.

I didn't have the time, nor did I care to cover my body from his eyes before he walked in. He was home early, then again, it could've been a Saturday or Sunday. Time wasn't my friend, nor was it my enemy, cause it just didn't exist.

"My God" he exhaled and I played with the water some more. "Was this from me?".

I looked up, both of us lookin' like a deer in headlights. I wanted to gag, it wasn't possible he could've forgotten this, all of it, was from him. He took off his jacket and kicked off his sandals before comin' into the bathroom.

He opened the glass shower door and I moved aside fer him as he shut off the water. He didn't say nothin', just stared at me with a closed fist in his mouth like he'd been caught in a fishin' trap. I pulled my knees close to my chest and picked away at the blue paint he put on my toes a few nights ago.

"June" he lifted my head with a finger. "I won't do this to ya no more, I'm sorry".

I let him cup my face and lift my lips to his like I wanted his comfort. He left me not long enough to grab the towel hangin' up on the door and he wrapped it around me. Rubbin' the dry fabric up and down my arms and legs how mama used to do when I was younger.

I didn't know what to say to him when he asked if I was alright, cause I wasn't. I found my days better spent as a zombie, a girl who was foolish enough to be at the wrong place at the wrong time.

I already forgot how he got me to the house, the maze I couldn't escape. I forgot why he picked cornfields and not a forest of trees. I forgot why he wanted me and why I didn't care fer him. I was mush, entirely a ball of oozin' lard laid as waste.

I let him pick me up, carry me to the bed. I let him pick out my clothes as winter ended long ago and spring was nearly finished too. He dressed me in jeans, a white t-shirt, and a black cardigan, tellin' me I'd fit in.

"Yer shoes are downstairs" he pulled away before he could kiss my lips.

"Why do I need shoes?".

"I'm takin' ya on vacation, my love" he helped me stand. "It's about time I get ya outta this house".

I tried to hide my surprise, but I wasn't good at that- like most things. So, I floated behind him like a curtain does in the wind as we made our way down the stairs. Things started to make sense; why he beat my body and stopped doin' my face up, why he starved me fer three days to make me weaker, why this did that and that did this.

I looked at my hands like a dumb fool and not my feet cause they were finally free and I couldn't even run. I was so exhausted, so tired, starved, and emaciated from the days before. I was so skinny, if I stood sideways and stuck out my tongue, I'd look like a zipper.

The livin' room was dark, same as the rest of the house, looked a lot cleaner too. There were secrets in this vacation, there was more than just him wantin' to take me somewhere. I shook my head and grabbed onto both sides, tryin' anythin' to get rid of the instigatin' pulse.

"Ready?" he grabbed my hands. "Ya ain't got nothin' to be afraid of, Junie, cars already packed with yer stuff and mine. Even got some snacks fer us to eat on the way, I know ya skipped yer meals".

I didn't know whether to pity him a smile or to pretend like I didn't hear him, so I did both. I let him walk me outside, more so because I needed it fer myself since I could hardly stand on my own. The door creaked open and I finally saw more, lightin' up my eyes like a single firework on the fourth of July.

The cold breeze hit my lungs like a brick to the head. I would've fallen down if not fer Hunter holdin' me up like I was his perfect porcelain doll.

"I'm sorry" I quickly said.

He let me go, locked the front door, and rest his head upon it with a heavy sigh.

"I should be the one apologizin' and not ya" he spun around and took my hands. "I ain't never brought ya outside, June. That's probably why you've been so sad this entire time. I know ya and yer mama always had fun outside in the garden and I completely held that from ya".

"It does feel nice" I admitted into the silence and whispered once more. "It feels- nice".

I hadn't been out, consciously at least, since I first got to the house. He let me go and motioned fer me to follow him to his new car. I looked between him and his truck, the long driveway passin' fields on fields of corn.

The cold air kissed my skin, sendin' shivers up and down my spine like I was alive again. It was the first time since forever that I was able to finally breathe fresh air. It was the first time I wasn't breathin' in the stench of repeated abuse, torture, and rape.

I thought about runnin', thought about pushin' as hard as I could while screamin' fer someone to help me. Mama was close, Abilene was close, Colton was closer than I thought. I stood there lookin' at Hunter, knowin' damn well he'd hurt me if I tried anythin' he told me not to.

I took off my shoes and told him I just wanted to feel the dirt on my feet. He laughed to himself and dropped his head before tellin' me he was the luckiest man to have me. I stepped down the three steps leadin' away from the covered porch that looked like it wrapped around the front and sides of the dark red house.

The ground was cold on my feet as I stepped through the dirt and sparse grass. Hunter held out his hand and I reached fer it, only cause I knew he saw my shakin' legs off balancin' my way. He was sweet durin' moments like this and I wondered if I could force myself to like him.

Then there were moments as the one I bit my tongue fer enjoyin'. My hair fell in front of my face as he steadied me and the moon illuminated his angry eyes. I wanted to ask what happened, what I did to cause him to change, but I knew better to leave him be.

He grabbed onto my neck and I cried out, he was gonna leave bruises, broken veins and marks fer everyone to see. I backed up until I couldn't no more and the tree that helped hold me dug its bark into my back. Fer sure he left lacerations and blood on the clothes I thought I'd be travelin' in.

He twirled my loose hair between his fingers, starin' down at me like I committed murder. He dropped my hair to caress my eyes, nose, and lips.

"I'm sorry, June" he dropped his head and reached into his pocket. "We ain't gonna be able to leave until tomorrow, there's one more thing I gotta do".

I kept my gaze on his until he pressed the needle deep into my neck, then my head shot up. Though full and bright fer my savior to ignore, the stars still wished me goodnight. They were full, my favorite part of the day, seein' them light up the sky in novas of hundreds.

My legs were the first to give out, then my eyes. I fumbled on words I didn't know how to form anymore, and I fumbled my hands around his arms. Hunter was whisperin' or screamin' somethin' at me that I couldn't hear. I told him I was sorry, I thought I did. I didn't mean to fall asleep when we were supposed to be leavin' so soon.

***

I had a dream I was underwater, swimmin' with dolphins and giant turtles that could swallow the sea. I was in the blue sky that birthed life and took it back just as quickly. Like a mother givin' her children room to grow, not tellin' them about the fenced cage they were in.

I had a dream I was with mama again, but she was mad at me. She was angry with me, tellin' the whole town it was my fault fer gettin' caught up with Hunter. She blamed me fer daddy leavin', said he never would've left if I would've kept quiet and been a good girl. She ain't explain more.

She sat in a rockin' chair, agin' like a pumpkin the day after Halloween, laughin' until her smile fell off. Mama's eyes got big like tears before fallin' from her face and they turned to smoke in the air. I called out fer mama, begged her to come back when she got up and flew away.

"You're dyin' baby girl" she whispered a kiss to my cheek.

My head smacked onto somethin' hard and a small chuckle escaped someone's dirty lips to my left. *Hunter*. He placed a hand on my head and wished me a good mornin'. My eyes slowly opened, closin' in record time cause of the light.

"There's Tylenol and a water to yer right, why don't ya take some? It'll help with yer headache and body aches".

The sun was piercin' down on me as I sat in the passenger side of his truck. He hit another bump in the road and my entire body shifted, causin' it to ache all over, especially in my neck and upper back. I grabbed onto the clear water and made note of my freshly painted soft pink nails.

He knew I hated pink, everythin' about it, and still, made me play dress up. My clothes were the same as yesterday's, just a grey shirt instead of white. I still wore a tight pair of jeans, black boots, and a black jacket fer the cold breeze I'm sure we'd have.

I looked back at Hunter calmly drivin', he was wearin' a forest green polo with dark blue jeans. His hair was gelled back too, and I wondered where he was takin' me, us. A searin' pain formed behind my eyes and I bit back a hiss as I started to remember the drug from the night before. After the incision, I was out.

I opened the brand-new bottle of Tylenol and I chugged down double the amount askin', just to make sure nothin' was gonna hurt later. The back of my head was achin' all up my spine and crown. I screwed the lid back on the water, placin' it on the ground, and I raised my hand to my head.

I audibly gasped and Hunter didn't even twitch, like he'd known what he done was wrong. I ripped the knitted black hat off my head and ran my fingers across every inch of my chopped hair.

"I didn't want to do it" Hunter looked at his watch. "I really didn't want to do it, but yer so beautiful and other people would've noticed".

I quickly snapped down the sun blocker and opened the mirror. Lookin' back at me was a stranger, someone I didn't recognize. I once had long black hair and tan skin, but not the face I now saw. She wore makeup too pale fer her skin, and her hair was cut short and dyed platinum to her shoulders.

My hazel eyes were once greener but now had far more brown imbalances paradin' around my irises. I couldn't stop feelin' the end of my hair, couldn't hold back them tears fer it too. I was fallin' apart, and now, I was unrecognizable.

"I'll miss yer natural hair too, but once we get back home I can dye it fer ya and we'll just have to wait fer it to grow back" he smiled like he'd done me a favor.

"When we get back".

He put his hand on my head and I slapped him away. His nostrils flared and his breathin' grew heavier, I felt like the worst person ever. I felt like I wasn't in my right mind to have done that and I should've known better.

"I'm sorry" I kissed his hand, tryin' not to gag. "It's just a little hard to get used to all the changes that have been happenin', especially when I don't know about them".

"It's fer yer own good, June" he smiled. "I appreciate ya apologizin', shows me I'm startin' to grow on ya".

I smiled, pushin' back tears and acted like the perfect girl he wanted. He'd been drivin' all day; told me I was actin' like a snake in the grass when I offered to drive. It was just a gesture; I knew I wasn't gettin' out anytime soon.

We stopped at a hotel, wasn't sure of the name cause I had to keep my cap on and my head low just to get in. He told me he had a gun, that he'd shoot everyone if I told them I needed help and who I was.

It was a poorly lit lobby, small too. Didn't surprise me though since we did stop in the middle of nowhere, where the population was probably less than my own hometown, which wasn't much.

"Fredrick and June Gainthers" Hunter said to the plump lady at the front desk.

"The newly engaged couple" she smiled, handin' him a pamphlet. "As a way for us to say congratulations, we've promoted you to the lovebirds special suite at no additional cost".

"My fiancé and I thank ya very much" he wrapped an arm 'round me, carryin' our bags in hand.

I smiled at the woman with a tear in my eye, hopin' she'd take the hint and ask if I was okay, just so I could lie and pretend I was. Just so I could show Hunter that I wasn't goin' to do nothin' to go against him.

Fer his trust.

"Hey, you look familiar, have we met?" she asked, gatherin' together the keys.

I stood cemented in my shoes, not knowin' if I could speak, what to say, what to do. I hadn't spoken to anyone in months and her voice was the first I heard as well.

"I-" I looked at Hunter to make sure it was okay to speak and he nodded. "I'm startin' to think everyone looks like everyone" I joked. "I look like someone's cousin, niece, friend, and dog!".

"You'd be surprised how often she gets that" Hunter added. "Now, if you'll excuse us".

He opened the door with a swipe of the blue card and I was surprised by the quality of the place. The bedroom was huge, with a king-sized bed in the middle against the wall. There were rose petals and a glass of champagne on one of the small tables in the kitchenette as well.

Hunter let me go and told me to explore, said I earned it fer bein' a good girl with the receptionist. I wandered in and out of the three rooms, tryin' to avoid Hunter when I could, but he started followin' me after unpackin' our bags.

"We'll be here two days" he leaned on the archway of the bathroom door. "Why don't we take a bath, huh?".

I looked at myself in that there mirror, watchin' a stranger play obedient to a dog. She had blonde hair, whiter skin, she had worry in her tired and dead eyes that screamed fer life to stop.

I stood and told him I was too tired, that I ain't wanna do nothin' but sleep. He smiled at the floor tellin' me not to test him, and there was nothin' I could do. He cut my hair, took my memories, and drugged me fer his use.

I even told him I was on my period, which was a lie, and even he knew it. Told me he'd been keepin' track. I backed away as he walked forward, cornerin' me. He stopped once he got to the bath and he turned it on. Hot steam soon filled the white tiled bathroom and he closed the door, lockin' it with a smirk.

"Come here" he gestured with his pointer finger. "Let me take care of ya".

I let him undress me, place kisses on my skin that shivered my core with poison, and then it was my turn. He postured up and waited fer me to unbutton his shirt, unzip his pants, and stand straight fer him to lift me up and place me in the large tub.

He soon followed, sittin' behind me and holdin' me up. It wasn't hard to not cry, I was too used to it by now. I knew what he wanted; it was my body. Never my thoughts, my intellect, nor was it my heart. He said he knew all those things of me, yet only wanted my skin on his hands.

"I like yer skin, I like how it feels under my hands" he bit my neck.

I let him have his way with me in that bathroom, tryin' not to move to make it less painful. It still hurt, every time he did what he wanted, I was in an unbearable amount of pain. I tried practicin' my breathin', countin' my abc's backwards to distract myself.

Nothin' worked.

It was my fault, that's what he said.

He was a kind lover, treated me nicely, that's what he said.

He wrapped his forearm over my neck and used the other to do the same across my stomach.

"I love ya" he squeezed my body. "I love ya more than ya will ever know".

It got to the point where I couldn't breathe. My vision spotted, and within five seconds, I was out. I woke up to him settin' me on the bed and tuckin' me under them sheets. He kissed my forehead and walked off in his naked skin towards the bathroom.

I placed a hand on my hot throat and cried silently to myself, fer I knew somethin' was gonna happen soon. I couldn't tell exactly what it was, but I was startin' to know him more than he could possibly know himself. He lived through his ego, and I was the mirror that saw through.

He was gone fer longer than expected, his trust in me was too much than what I had to give. My heart was tellin' me not to do it, God it was beggin' me to stop the itch and to lay down in the bed. To do whatever I needed to do to please him to live till tomorrow.

I did somethin' bad while he was finishin' up in the bathroom. I grabbed the phone near the bedside and I called the front desk number sketched onto the room key. I waited and waited fer it to ring, but nothin' happened.

"I'm not sure if you can hear me" I whispered into the phone. "My name is Millie Maye and I've been kidn-".

"What are ya doin?" Hunter crawled in bed.

I slammed the phone down and faced him with stutterin' lips. He grabbed onto my tremblin' chin and soothed my cries by tellin' me to shut up and take responsibility fer what I did.

"I didn't mean-" I tried comin' up with an excuse.

"So yer tellin' me that the phone magically fell into yer hands? And it just so happened to already be ringin' the receptionist? It's okay, June. I unplugged the phones as soon as we got here, no one heard ya".

No one heard me.

Hello, to the empty promises I made to mama.

"But now, you've really made me sad" he rotated on top and pinned me down. "I sure hoped you'd behave durin' our trip, but it seems like yer gonna make this hard on me, aren't ya love?".

I felt spiders crawl all over my body as he laid on top with his dry skin and hairy chest pressed against my breasts and stomach. He told me I felt good when he explored my flesh with his fingers. I pushed him away and tried to sit up, but he threw my face hard onto the bed, grippin' my hands above my head.

"Hunter, please" I cried. "It hurts".

"It ain't hurtin' me, June" he bit my lip, drawin' blood.

Then he bit my neck, my breasts, my stomach, thighs, knees, and shins. Then he kissed my lips, neck, breasts, stomach, thighs, knees, and shins. I was squirmin' too much fer his likin', causin' too much of a distraction.

He called me a bitch and pulled out his gun from the other side of the bed. He made me open my mouth and bite down on the barrel. I was shakin' too much from it though, my heart was poundin' throughout my whole body, but he told me it felt better when I did.

I prayed to God fer him to not shoot, I prayed and prayed to God and my savior fer someone to interfere. I even asked the heavens to kill Hunter so I would no longer think about it fer myself.

They answered with torture, with more pain. He positioned himself between my legs, cuppin' my face with the gun in hand, and workin' himself like he was somethin' I wanted. I couldn't even cry out cause he stuffed some of the blankets into my mouth.

He dropped the gun and wrapped his hands tight around my neck, growin' my vision spotty and swearin' at me every time I coughed. I could hardly breathe, feel, live.

The last things I remembered was him on me, sweat drippin' from his nose and onto my face, my body rockin' back and forth without me havin' to do nothin', and the sound of the bed's backboard vigorously hittin' the wall.

There was nothin' keepin' me goin' as I laid there submissive, but the broken promise of seein' mama again, even though some days I didn't want to.

I was too damaged fer her to want me back.

CHAPTER X

"June! June!" Hunter called from the food truck.

I could barely sit up straight; he drugged me each day we left the hotel room. I didn't even know what day it was, nor could I recollect how many days we'd been gone fer. I was a scarecrow, stuffed up on drugs and broken glass, breakin' bones every second I had.

He poised me up against the metal chair overlookin' the Gulf of Mexico. It was beautiful, but I was in no mind or body to appreciate it fer what it was. Colton said he'd bring me here, so I did my best to pretend it was him and not Hunter.

As I always did.

"I got ya a corndog, love" he moved the fried hair away from my eyes and lowered my hat over my face. "Gotta stay down, remember?".

A warm breeze flew our napkins off the small table and across the dinin' area. I listened as seagulls laughed and waves crashed over one another in dispute. The sand looked invitin', the others must've thought the same too.

Even if I wanted, I couldn't splash 'round in the water cause my legs wouldn't move like that fer me. Hunter was pushin' me 'round in a wheelchair, receivin' pitied smiles from strangers walkin' by. I hoped he wouldn't get used to the idea and permanently cause me to be like this forever.

I stared at the food in front of me with a watered mouth, quite possibly even droolin', but there was nothin' I could do about it. Hunter wrapped his warm hand around mine and gave me a smile, usin' his other hand to grab the plastic knife.

God I was havin' sinful thoughts while he cut the corndog into tiny bits I could swallow. I was just picturin', just hopin', to get my sober hands on that there plastic knife so I could feel it stabbin' through his skin.

He raised the fork to my mouth and I struggled to open, chewin' lightly on the piece though I wanted to scarf it down. Them drugs were workin' my body so much it left me too tired to do anythin' but breathe. I was startin' to get worried Hunter would attach a feedin' tube to me.

"Ya know" he leaned in to whisper. "If ya were a good girl, I ain't have to do this to ya, love".

It was hard fer me to talk with everythin' inside me as it was, so I bugged my eyes in fear I didn't have to pretend existed, and I swallowed my food hard. He dropped his head with a smile and a chuckle I never found attractive, tellin' me I was adorable like *this*.

I closed my eyes when I finished my food, still hungry, still unable to speak my wants though I never would. I read a book once about a girl that fell in love with her abductor, they called in Stockholm syndrome.

Lookin' at the fool sittin' cross from me, I knew it was never gonna happen. Quite bluntly made me realize more of what I wanted in life, and that, was what I already had before. I wondered if Abe made new friends, if she went off to college and where. I wondered if Colton found love in another's eyes or if he really was waitin' fer me.

I tried picturin' what it'd be like.

I came home from college, roses scattered across the floor of mine and Colton's home. We were engaged not too long ago, singin' everyday fer the blessins' the Lord showered us with. I followed them roses into the hall and then the bath.

Candles were lit, beautiful drops of lavender and eucalyptus steamed from the tub he made fer me. Even had piano music playin' in the background. He walked in after me, placin' kisses on my neck and tellin' me to relax.

Every week he did this fer me, every week he revived my soul. When I wanted to be alone, he left. When I wanted his love, companionship, and memory, he came. I was entirely in control, breathin' the life I knew he wanted fer me, fer the both of us.

We lived two towns over, had lots of land, even started tryin' fer our own kin. Didn't take long fer the first, and then the other two. Colton even expanded our home, addin' on three rooms and a large gatherin' space fer our family's nightly prayer hour.

It was beautiful, our life.

It wasn't real.

"Are ya fakin' with me?" Hunter ripped me from the deep sleep I hadn't realized I fell into.

"I'm sorry" I barely spoke with a coarse throat. "I didn't mean to-".

"It's okay" he smiled, unbucklin' my seatbelt.

My body jolted upright with new movements, slowly awakenin' from a week's worth of drug abuse and other actions I didn't quite care to speak of. I looked 'round the empty lot we parked at, bein' the only car there.

We were surrounded by woods, forests I believed existed in other states. Made me wonder just where we were, knowin' I could never ask Hunter that question. The sun was soon settin' too, makin' me feel like I was at my final destination.

Everythin' was alive though. Lilacs bloomed off in the distance and small yellow seeds blossomed into beautiful flowers I didn't know the names of. The forest was smilin' with life of green leafed trees, rich evergreens, and hundreds of ferns scattered about the floor.

"I ain't gonna hurt ya, darlin'. Just wanna take ya on a walk" he picked up my body like it was made of air.

"I can't walk" I gripped onto his arms before realizin' I was standin' well enough on my own.

I gave him a questionin' look before he had the chance to wrap his arms 'round me and pull me in close. I pretended his warmth was Colton's, pretended the peck on my head was his lips and not Hunters. It was easier to get by when I pretended his body wasn't his, just as mine wasn't mine either.

I smelt rain in the air, crisp and fresh. The hairs on my skin stood and my body started healin' itself by usin' them energies in the land.

He didn't say nothin' after he held my arm and stumblin' body, draggin' me off the forest trail and into unmarked territory. I was whiplashed, movin' left and right, up and down, even my clothes dirtied and tore without my control or say.

The air was wet, moist even as it danced over my bare shoulders and legs, frizzin' my short hair, and heatin' my skin. I knew I looked a hot mess, but I didn't care, especially when a crack from far away stood Hunter straight.

"Ya keep yer trap shut, got it?" he yelled an angry whisper into my hair.

I crouched low behind fallen trees and tall ferns, knowin' my new outfit hid me perfectly as camouflage. Sometimes I think I underestimated Hunter and the things he did, but I had to hand it to him, he was smart. He knew just about everythin' about everyone and everythin'.

Two people, a couple, came into view. Seemed like they were headin' away from a romantic spot they created memories in. I hummed to myself and wondered what it was like to give consent of your body away to someone like that.

It took only a few moments fer them to loose themselves in the forest and away from where we were headin'. Hunter grabbed me by the hand again, squeezin' hard and sayin' he was sorry. I followed him past turns, animal paths, and over streams until he stopped.

Thorn bushes, ferns, and giant pines surrounded us in a crowd of mystery. Even as the sun faded and the moon began its ascent, I felt at ease. If I were to die, everythin' would stop. Surely investigators would find my body and mama could finally be at ease. Surely there'd be enough DNA in and all over my body fer the police to know it was Hunter.

"We're here" he smiled, lettin' go to rest his back on a tree.

I watched him not move or make another sound. He was too busy watchin' me with curious eyes, wonderin' if I figured out the secret to the questions I didn't understand. He opened his mouth to speak, but quickly closed it with a smack and a smile.

"I don't understand" I whispered. "What are you showin' me?".

He scratched his growin' hair and pushed off the tree, walkin' behind it. He poked his hand out from the other side and motioned with one finger fer me to follow. I contemplated runnin' away, but I didn't know where I was and I knew damn well he'd find me just like he did time after time.

"I told ya I'd protect ya, didn't I?" he plucked my head from my neck and pointed my eyes down.

I didn't understand what I was supposed to be lookin' at and I told him that again, only givin' him a spoken signal to laugh about somethin' I lost.

"June, meet Timothy" he chuckled.

I lost my breath, took a step back, hittin' my back against a tree. I asked what he said, and without shame or guilt, he told me he buried my rapist there, under the ground I stood on. Told me it took him almost all night cause the ground was cold and he had to make sure no one saw him.

"I can't even begin to imagine what they must be feelin' right now" mama paused between breaths. "They don't even know where their son is. I'd much

rather wanna know if he was dead or not instead of havin' to guess".

I watched mama flip off the station to one of her beloved soap operas, takin' a big pause before startin' up another conversation with me.

"I don't want you endin' up like that boy from yer school".

"You won't have nothin' to worry about" I lied, swallowin' a lump in my throat.

I knew what I said could've been a lie, and yet, I did nothin' to stop it. I didn't tell mama, when I sure as hell should've. I didn't tell Colton when he kissed away my tears and held me tenderly under the blankets while we watched movies on his couch.

It was my fault why things went too far. It was my fault and I was to blame. I told no one. I told not a single soul and on my dead body and mama's tears, I was gonna suffer fer it. Shit on me cause I was the damned fool.

"I did this fer ya" he kissed my tears.

"I never asked fer this. I never asked fer any of this".

"June, ya don't mean that, my love" he pulled me in, kissin' my lips.

"Get away from me and rot in hell, Hunter Davis" I pushed him away, takin' off fer the woods.

I could run, I was runnin'. I was a fool smilin' as I was, not knowin' what the hell was gonna happen to me if he caught me. My legs were like gazelles in Africa, hopin' the lion couldn't see in the dark and was full from his other meals.

"June" he roared through the plains.

Don't say a word, don't bat an eye, run like I was goin' to die.

Cause I was.

Branches smacked my face as my beatin' heart exploded from my chest and ran off without me. I asked it to come back, but it couldn't hear me over my heavy breathin'. I thought I was gonna pass out. My body was so weak. My mind was so weak.

Small ferns and twigs cracked under my feet and thorns tore at my exposed ankles. I was bleedin' real bad, even cut my hand on a broken branch. I heard him chasin' after me, thought his voice trampled close behind, but I was divinely mistaken.

"Hello?" a husk voice called.

I stopped in my tracks, watchin' my soul keep on runnin' before realizin' we stopped and she came back. Maybe if I kept on goin', maybe if I didn't stop, things would be different. The man showed himself to me, even came near when I told him to stay back.

He was tall, large, and plump. It was hard to see him without the sun, but the warmth of his fire showed me he was a kind soul campin' alone in the woods. I let him help me up, even told him he wasn't safe.

He took off his red flannel and wrapped it 'round my bare shoulders. I thanked him and told him again with urgency he had to leave, that he'd find me.

"What are you runnin' from?" he asked, lookin' 'round the area.

"My name is Millie Maye" I grabbed onto his strong arms. "Please help me".

"You're that kid that went missin' last year, ain't you?" his eyes widened. "I'm goin' to call the police".

"No, there's no time. Do you have a car?" freedom was finally singin'. "We have to leave no-".

There was a hard knock and I fell. My entire body was numb, paralyzed by a blunt so forced I thought I died. I knew I was cryin', whimperin' too when his silhouette danced in front of my eyes. He was laughin' like a fool, high on my pain once again.

My body was growin' cold, couldn't even move it if I wanted to. Cause there Hunter was, sittin' on top of me, bashin' my head in with some unfortunate rock he found on the quiet forest floor. I was gonna look unrecognizable in my casket.

"Oh God" he stopped; mouth muffled, battlin' the song of heaven's angels. "I'm so- June- I love y-".

My skin viciously turned cold as ice; I was all alone. I think Hunter ran off somewhere without me. Blood was seepin' up my throat and out my mouth, I couldn't stop gaspin'. My arms and legs twitched too; I would've laughed if I didn't think I was gonna die.

I felt my blood mixin' in with the cold and damp soil. I squeezed some in my hand, tryin' to feel anythin' before lights went out.

People ran past me; I think I asked fer their help. People ran past me; they didn't care I was dyin'. I heard a body fall, sounded like a tree comin' down hard.

"Please help me" the man screamed. "I'm at the-".

His voice cut off, dead end.

Dead.

God was I cold, yet my soul warmin' up to take me someplace I'd been dreamin' about goin' fer, how long did he say? A year. Cause that's how long I'd been gone fer. I swallowed some blood, spittin' it back up and I laid there, cause there was nothin' else I could do.

Lights poured in beautifully around my body and I was carried by the hands of a thousand angels. Each one sung a tune, a lullaby, to keep me from askin' questions. Each one kissed my eyes closed and told me to rest.

I think I saw granddaddy on mama's side. He was always my guardian angel, that's what mama told me. I met him two days after I was born, he died later that day. Mama said he waited real hard just to see me with his own eyes.

I only saw what he looked like through pictures, he's who I got my dark hair and tan skin from. I had him to thank fer the full head of hair. I smiled, runnin' into his arms as I shrunk to the size of a three-year-old.

He scooped me up and told me he loved me. I asked him what I was doin' there, I didn't understand. I had no memories of the life before, except fer him. He told me somethin' happened to me and I had to leave earth fer a quick second, but that I'd have to go back.

I was a kid, cryin' in his arms, tellin' and demandin' him that I stay. I told him life was a lot harder than I thought it was before signin' up fer it. He threw me in the air, grew a large pair of sapphire wings, and caught me before I fell.

"Your mama needs you, little peanut" he kissed my soft hair and rubbed his thumb across my forehead.

My stomach turned and my memories of him in the afterlife dispersed like fireflies runnin' away from each other too quickly. I tried grabbin' onto the scattered pieces of him, but they went through my hands as I became physically heavy in heaven's clouds.

My body fell, I was fallin' fast towards earth. I raised my hands to protect my face, and soon the earth opened her mouth and swallowed me whole, birthin' me again through her tunnel.

My head jerked upright, releasin' a loud and muffled scream from my torn lips. Dried blood softened and wet the entirety of my esophagus, makin' it harder to breathe. I tried movin', tried gettin' away, but I was stuck.

Somethin' was holdin' me tight to the tree behind me, proppin' me up and straight. They wrapped over the bones of my hips, held my arms down, crossed over my neck, and tied tightly just under my jaw.

"Shh, June, it's okay" Hunter dropped everythin' in his sticky hands to smooth my hair and wipe away my tears. "I promise ya, everythins' gonna be okay. I lost my temper back there. I'm sorry, my love".

He kissed my forehead and I wished I could've seen his face, but there ain't no light fer that. I didn't even think he knew what he was doin' given how dark the sky was. Even the stars didn't feel like gracin' us with their beauty.

He rustled with somethin' in his pocket before clippin' it onto the front of my restraints, and he turned it on. A faint light escaped and illuminated just enough fer me to know I was out fer much longer than I should've been.

Hunter smiled before jumpin' into the large hole he dug with a shovel from only God knows where. It was already dug past his height, makin' it deeper than six feet. He was gonna bury me dead or alive.

I squirmed 'round and tried screamin', knowin' no one could help me.

"June, check it out" he popped out his head, holdin' somethin' white. "My name's Tim".

He crawled out of the hole I now knew was a grave, bringin' the skull close to my face. Hunter said it was Tim, told me if I didn't behave, he was gonna make him bite me. All why laughin'; the psychopath threw the skull back into the grave and marched towards me again.

"Please" I muffled, yet nothin' but an agonized moan escaped.

"June, don't worry" he moved the blood dried hair behind my ear. "This ain't fer ya".

I followed his eyes towards a shadow in the near distance. It was large and familiar. Hunter dropped his head and told me it was my fault, that I should've been more well behaved and nothin' like this would've happened.

If I knew nothin', but one thing, I knew more than ever that I was responsible for that man's death. The man campin' alone, thinkin' he could help a poor girl like me. I was no better than them people helpin' bring children over to the islands of rich folk.

He grabbed the dead and frozen man by his ankles, draggin' him to the side of the grave.

"Ya couldn't have picked a smaller person?" he laughed.

The body rolled into the grave with a few tough shoves, soundin' a wave once he hit the bottom. Hunter asked if I wanted to say any last words fer my new friend. I simply shook my head and cried relief cause I wasn't gonna die.

I was selfish.

And I cried again and again cause I knew I was never gonna escape him.

Ever.

Hunter finished up buryin' the body, just in time too cause the sun was beginnin' to rise. He told me we had to hurry and gave me no time to help myself. He picked me up and ran while carryin' me to his car, throwin' me into the passenger side before anyone could spot us.

He changed his shirt and poured water over his hands to clean em' of all the blood before washin' his face and gettin' into the car.

"I almost forgot" he pulled out a knife from his pocket.

He held it close to my face and I pulled away. He bit his bottom lip and swore, tellin' me he wasn't gonna hurt me. I sickly believed him because I knew his love fer me was far different than anythin' I ever experienced. I was gonna have to learn how to deal with it on my own.

Just the two of us.

Forever.

Just as he wanted.

Just the two of us.

Forever.

I wasn't sure how long he'd been drivin' fer, but we passed many cars, cities, towns, and everythin' it seemed. I was still tied up, wearin' the red flannel of a man I didn't mean to kill.

I replayed his voice in my head, rewatched my pleadin' fill his thoughts, give him hope that he could help me. I was a fool.

We never went back to the hotel, yet all of our things were back in the car. I think Hunter was smarter than I thought, like I had said he was. I just had to say it again, cause everyday he gathered our things in case we had to run. I'm sure he bleached everythin' too before leavin'.

I woke up with tired and swollen eyes, tryin' to see past the dim lights of his headlights that looked across the dead and dark highway. Hunter's hand was on my inner thigh, I think that's what initially woke me up. My mouth was no longer gagged, yet I knew I couldn't speak.

My head pulsated and blood still trickled down my neck. Iron covered me and I looked at Hunter. He swore under his breath and told me to stop bleedin', that there wasn't anythin' he could do fer me in that sense. Told me if I hadn't run, he wouldn't have had to do it.

I stared at him not knowin' what to think. That deranged animal was far from sane, and I was the only one who was gonna know. My stomach turned and hot acid came up my throat. I puked up my entire existence onto the floor of his car and he swerved to the side of the road.

Thank God no one else was drivin', otherwise I was gonna be blamed fer their death too. He parked near tall shrubs far away and turned off the car. I watched him from outside of my body, like I was watchin' a movie. Granddaddy was there holdin' my hand on the body that wasn't my body, but floatin' eyes.

Hunter carried me outta the car and far into the open field of a farmer who should've cut down his dead crops by now.

My body couldn't move, breathe, or do anythin' when he laid me down in the hidden spot. I wasn't cotton pickin', nor was I havin' a ball. Existin' wasn't even close either.

"Yer not feelin' well, love" he held me down hard, stabbin' dried twigs into my back.

"Why can't you just die? Why won't you die already?" I managed to cry through broken screams. "I-just-want-you-to-go".

He smoothed a finger over my restraints, loosenin' them around my breasts and between my legs. He tore open my shirt and used his pocket knife to cut a hole in the tight jeans I thought were a barrier from him.

"Don't tease me like this" he unzipped his pants. "Ya know how it makes me feel, how it gets us both goin', June".

CHAPTER XI

Spiders in my hair, centipedes in my bones, worms and maggots diggin' through my flesh like I ain't still alive. It's almost like I can taste their whispers on my skin, each one singin' fer my death to permeate itself.

I can't breathe in the underworld; I can't sleep either. I have no use fer this body, and even the devil knows it. I never met him, but I could laugh at that cause I had.

Every night and every mornin' he'd visit my cage. He'd poke at the metal walls and tell me to sing fer him, and I'd do it.

I ain't nothin' but a coward.

"Millie Maye?" a voice creeped up from underneath me. "It's been too long".

I couldn't move, the compacted dirt held me down in that there grave, turnin' me to stone. I called out, tellin' them to leave me alone. Not again. I didn't want to see them, him, again. Cause of what happened, the same skeleton with curious bones kept torturin' me.

"There you are" the bones from his fingers poked through his grave and into mine. "My friend".

I screamed, dirt poured into my mouth, his fingers followed and I choked on his bones. He thrust his hand far down my throat; I lost my eyes and the darkened underworld turned black. I couldn't see, feel, nor hear my own body.

"Don't be afraid, I just wanna touch ya".

His skeleton oozed into mine, tanglin' our corpses like we'd been birthed from the same womb. I prayed to one of the three dogs of Hades to play fetch with him, and if not, with me. If I pushed, my hands sunk through his chest and past his bones.

He tilted my head back and bit my neck, I didn't even bleed. I screamed, clawed, fought with everythin' I had to get outta there. A little girl called my name, called me mama. I thought she was me, callin' out fer my own mama.

My dream ended, that's where it always cut off at. I didn't like not knowin' who she was. Fer the past few weeks, she'd been callin' me mama. I was her, callin' out fer my own mama. Made me wonder if I'd see mama soon.

I closed my eyes weeks later and the bones of Timothy Handerthorn pinned me down once more. If I weren't dead already, I'd be soon. If in my dreams I could no longer escape, sleep, come back to life, I would never do it in the wakin' world.

There I was, back in the devil's home, six feet under with no light, love, or purpose. There I was, tortured, abused, and raped, fer showin' the wrong person kindness. I ain't nothin' but a trailer trashed washed up reject.

The bones of his hand were caressin' my cheek, he thought he was soothin' away my tears so he could get some later. Later was too soon and I was in pain. I asked him to stop, told him I didn't want him. I even cried out fer Hunter.

He never came, the nights I asked him to stay. He was tired of me, I guess I caused him a lot of trouble those few weeks ago in the woods. I guess he had to go back and take care of some things without me.

That's why I slept fer so long. Think he induced some kinda long-term sleep within me. But I knew he was back already. I heard him when my mind wasn't awake, my thoughts unclear, and my eyes shut tighter than an Oklahoma window preparin' fer a storm.

He bit me again, tore off my lips so my cries muffled. Nothin' made it easier; thanks be to God I didn't have to see him. Them words left my voice too soon. I'm crazy.

His soulless eyes met my face and he forced his hands around my neck, makin' me look right at him. I was his puppet. Play me on a set of strings, please. God, I cried and I cried. There ain't nothin' I could've done to deserve God's love.

Not until I heard her little voice, one last time.

"Mama?".

I felt her walkin' 'round my grave, tellin' me to have courage. I faced the hollowed eyes of the man who stole me away one night and paid his dues. I told him it wasn't my fault, that he was the bad man takin' advantage of me.

I swore at him when he tried pullin' me down, but I was gettin' stronger. I was climbin' towards the heavens. Clawin' through layers and layers of broken promises to myself. Dirt, rocks, and everythin' snagged under my nails.

Rippin' them off, I left em' in a glorified blood bath. I didn't need em', just wanted my life. His lengthy fingers again came at my burnin' flesh, fallin' off at the ankles. I kicked him, sinkin' just a little bit deeper down. He kept screamin' like it was my fault.

And I fell, further down that grave and into the rabbit hole just before the devil's cave.

"Mama?".

Her little hand sliced through that blackened world like Archangel Michael's sword, lightin' up everythin' I had. She reached fer me, she chose me.

And I knew.

I was not forgotten.

"It was your fault" I spit at the lyin' corpse as I reached fer my savior's small hands.

I grabbed onto her little fingers, and with the helpful grace of God, they pulled me out.

I shot up, grabbin' my heart, I couldn't breathe. Throat felt fuzzy too. The sun hadn't rose through the slit of a window, so I tumbled on my toes towards the small bath. As soon as I got to that toilet, my body knew. I barely had time to lift the lid before I was hurlin'.

I wasn't sure how long I spent in that bathroom, didn't even hear Hunter when he walked in.

"What's the matter with ya?" he leaned on the archway.

I looked up at him, hair fallin' slightly in my face as I did. He smiled, walked towards me like he was gonna kiss me. I had somethin' to say, but my stomach had other thoughts and I threw up all inside that bowl.

"Let me help" he whispered, holdin' back my hair.

I raised a hand, hopin' he'd stay away, but I think it enticed him to follow more. He intertwined his fingers in mine and kissed the back of my hand like he owned it. Luckily fer me, my initial response was to throw up, and that's exactly what I did that entire mornin'.

Hunter got up and left sometime later, tellin' me he had to run to the store. He chained up one ankle, kissed my head, and locked my bedroom door before leavin' me completely. I waited till I could no longer hear his footsteps before gettin' up.

My shaky hands positioned themselves on both sides of the sink, liftin' my body ever so delicately. I stared at the beginnin' of the drain until I was bold enough to see her, to face her and tell her I was completely out of options. That I had no idea what to do.

My eyes were dull, my skin was flushed cold and white like a ghost I'd only just begun to see again. I raised a hand to the glass and outlined the unsettlin' color of my hair. It had already grown past my shoulders from the weeks after our *vacation*, displayin' the perfect line of bleached hair meets dark brown.

Despite the days and weeks I couldn't remember, I looked well-fed with no recollection. My stomach was firmer, growin' just a bit, so were my breasts. I wanted to wonder, create horrendous assumptions, yet my body stopped myself from doin' so.

I fell back to the toilet and spent the remainder of my day spittin' up acid then air. Ain't nothin' else was hurryin' to come out, so I didn't even try forcin' nothin'. Just told myself to enjoy the time I had to myself.

I closed my eyes, let my face rest on the seat, and soon the world went black. I no longer dreamed about bein' buried however many feet under, nor did I ever see the skeleton of Timothy Handerthorn again.

I was on a boat, rocked away, headin' towards shore to finally drop my anchor. I think my body was lettin' me know I could finally rest if I behaved well enough. If only I wasn't so stupid though. I knew everythin' was a fantasy when I woke up once more, not cradled before God's golden gates.

"It's okay, my love" Hunter wiped away the afternoon's tears.

My eyes opened to a poorly lit room, but I think it was supposed to be that way. Hunter helped me sit up straight, knowin' my stomach would turn again to spite me. I tried runnin' fer his bathroom, but he was quick enough to place a small waste bin in front of me.

He lifted my head, wiped my lips, and let me continue that process three or four or five more times. God I prayed fer some kind of peace to keep me from heavin'. I'd never felt so sick in my life, even with the previous drugs he wasted on me.

"Now I know it wasn't entirely my fault" he whispered with a kiss on my head.

"What?" I hurled once more. "What are you talkin' about?".

Though I could hardly see his face, I knew he was starin' at me with a mouthful of words he wanted to say. I let him help me sit up again, havin' him readjust the pillow, take the waste bin, and sit himself to my side.

"Come on, June" he smiled. "Let me show ya somethin' worthwhile".

He crawled out of bed and left fer the bathroom, comin' back almost instantly with somethin' small in his hands. If I hadn't known any better, I would've said it was a toothbrush. But I did know better, I stupidly knew what was happenin' to me and I wanted to avoid it all together.

"I knew it was gonna happen at some point" he handed me the pregnancy test.

I had no words, no surprises, nor did I have the world topplin' excitement that most women had when they found out there's a baby in their stomach. I blinked, stared, swallowed down everythin' I had as those two red lines screamed horrific notes at my face.

Hunter rustled in the sheets, pullin' them over my legs and slippin' a hand under the back of my shirt. His warm and bare hands glided all across my skin, sendin' shivers of horror throughout my body.

"Aren't ya excited?" he leaned and kissed my stomach. "We're finally gonna have the family we've always wanted".

He waited fer a response, though I was in no peace of mind to give him one. I ain't want none of anythin' he was givin' me. I ain't want nothin' but the childlike promises of Colton and whatever fairytales we made up with one another.

"Why am I so calm about all of this?" I said to the air and laughed.

"Because it's what ya want" he kissed my forehead.

"No" I said too fast, too harsh. "Not at all".

He pinched his lips, scooted off the bed, and stood by the door. Said somethin' about makin' us dinner, plumpin' me up, and puttin' a smile on my face. I didn't even acknowledge him and he still acted as if I had before leavin'. He was cynical. He was happier than a dead pig in the sunshine.

I put my hands on my belly, tryin' to feel the life that was supposedly in there. I sighed to myself and frustratingly knew I could've done better. God, why was I still beatin' myself up about somethin' I ain't have no control over?

I had no purpose in this life, no use fer myself. There ain't nothin' anyone could've said that'd make me feel like everythin' I'd been through and would have to endure was fer a good cause. I'd shit on em' if I ever heard em' say that to my face.

If I ever got out.

"Why?" I asked it. "Why did you have to come?".

I spent hours talkin' to myself, no, I spent hours talkin' to myself and the baby that was now inside of me. I tried rememberin' how long it had been since Hunter last raped me. I was pathetic, unable to even recall that.

I was his sleepin' beauty.

I went through my thoughts, memories, every audio file that had no video attachment. I was a broken record, reaskin' the same questions I had no authority in even askin'. I saw it though, it was gonna happen at some point.

Why couldn't it be the guy and not the girl that gets screwed over in the end? I could've used it against him, made him weak, vulnerable even. I could've waited fer his stomach to grow past his toes, unable to walk, run, stand up on his own.

God, I could've destroyed him.

So there I was, now layin' on the floor, starin' up at the star filled sky through the window. I could smell the food from down below too. My stomach growled and I protested against it, tellin' myself to have control, to stop bein' so selfish.

Hunter barged in before I could pretend like I wasn't doin' nothin', though I'm sure he already knew. What was there fer me to do except wait fer him to get in the mood, not care about me, and have his way? I wasn't essentially, but I was, his doll.

"Dinner's ready" he placed a kiss on my cheek.

No chains today as he helped me down the steep stairs near his bedroom door. The upstairs was created in a hurry, there was no doubt. But with each new week, he finished just a bit more. I was afraid of what was gonna happen once everythin' was completely built.

Would he want me more?

The lights were off, candles were lit everywhere. He was tryin' to make things romantic. He was tryin' to make me fall in love with him. What jokes arrived in the moments I was meant to be serious.

He covered my eyes with his hands and I took a sharp breath in. He told me to relax, that he had a surprise fer me.

"I wasn't sure what ya could stomach, so I made it all" he gave me back my sight.

The table was covered in fall foods and I wondered if time had already past and fell into fall. I thought that was a funny joke. Even then, had my birthday passed? I sat gently so he could push the chair in at the same time and he placed a cloth napkin on my lap.

It smelt amazin', delicious even, but I hadn't wanted him to see the satisfaction in my eyes. I pretended like it was vial, the worst stench I had ever come across. He told me he'd scrap it all if it made me feel better, but I held a hand fer him to hush up.

I ate in silence, zoned out from whatever it was he was sayin' to me. I was too busy focusin' on my meal, my first sober day, and the fact that I was pregnant. I was tryin' to figure out if the little girl askin' fer her mama was me or the baby inside.

I pretended to laugh at his jokes, might've even actually did at one fer real. I think he noticed, cause his smile widened like I'd never seen it, and he told me he was happy.

"I know what I did wasn't necessarily the best" he admitted. "But I want ya to know that I'm sorry, and I'm gonna spend the rest of my life tryin' to make it up to ya".

I took the last few bites of my food, tryin' to savor and enjoy as much of it as I could before I knew he'd lock me back up. The dinin' room was open fer the most part, a place I actually enjoyed most outta the entire room.

I raised the fork to my lips and the startlin' sound of a loud knock on the door made me drop it. I still remember the warmth comin' from the food as it just barely touched my lips. The fork flew out of my hands, chippin' the side of my plate, and landin' on the rug beneath us.

"Go upstairs, June" he whispered. "Go on".

I didn't realize what was happenin' until they knocked on the front door again. These were unexpected guests to Hunter. I swore they said his name, asked if he was home, and knocked even harder when the man of the house had nothin' to say.

"Hunter Davis" a rough voice yelled.

A rough voice.

Familiar.

Home.

"I said go-up-stairs" Hunter demanded, sharpenin' his tone with every word.

My eyes bugged, I contemplated jumpin' outta my skin just to get to that door before he could. *Colton.* We stood at the same time. My heart racin' a hundred miles per second.

My skin was itchin' to be freed. I opened my mouth to scream, too slow.

He put the barrel of his gun into my mouth and I bit my broken cry away. There was another knock on the door, and then another, and another. Hunter's hair fell in front of his crazed eyes and he lifted a finger to his lips to silence me.

I shook my head, tears pourin' from my eyes I could hardly see. I never wanted the knockin' on that door to stop, I never wanted to forget the sound of Colton's hands so close to my own. If only I could let him know I was there.

"I love ya" Hunter mouthed.

He removed the barrel from my mouth, instantly replacin' it with his hands. He stood behind me, draggin' me backwards up the stairs. The arm around my throat grew tighter the more I moved, the more I struggled to free myself.

"Hunter Davis" Colton yelled from behind the door. "This is the police".

My heart grew, his voice gave me strength. I bit my pride and threw my head back, knockin' a split in his lip and crunchin' his nose. He pissed a million swears under his breath. His arms were tight, I didn't even have to breathe, the blood wasn't goin' to my brain no more.

Slowly, the candles burned to the ground, the knockin' stopped, and my soul was put to rest. I woke up on the floor, mouth gagged and tapped over. The unfinished floors told me I was in my room, and the rattlin' chains meant I wasn't gettin' out anytime soon.

Sharp pains bugged from the backs of my eyes, out my nose, and all throughout my head. I knew already I was loosin' blood; I knew already I wasn't ever gonna heal that gouge in the back of my head before dyin'.

There weren't nothin' much fer me to do except cry. I laid there on that cold and rough floor, puttin' splinters in my skin just tryin' to crawl towards the door I'd never be able to open on my own.

I inched like a factory worm, overworkin' myself just to find it hadn't been closed all the way. I scrapped my head on the floor just to get a better listen to them. Just to see if I screamed, how muffled it would be and if anyone could hear me.

"They found Millie's blood in them woods" a man I didn't know spoke.

"What's this gotta do with me?" Hunter asked. "Millie is dead, it's time everyone and her mama put an end to this whole charade".

"You damn bastard" Colton yelled. "We know damn well you were there just last month doing God knows what".

Of course they found my blood. Maybe God did have a plan after all. I hadn't wanted another injury, but I also had no other way of lettin' people know where I was. I didn't care if I died at that point, just wanted someone to know the truth of what happened.

I didn't mean to leave mama behind.

"I've been goin' there every month since I was fifteen, officer" Hunter said sarcastically. "I can prove it to ya if ya want".

Their voices muffled into screams, movin' away from the front door. I wanted more, needed to hear more about the updates to my case, the man who left his entire campsite and was never found, and how mama was doin'.

I was selfish, unwisely selfish, and I did myself a terrible deed. I pushed off them chains, they pulled me back and my head split the door, closin' it hard. I couldn't hear nothin' no more, not even if I tried. More muffled screams piled on each other and I was forgotten about.

So I thought.

Their boots loudly slammed up the stairs, openin' my eyes and tellin' me to do somethin'. I tried to scream, I really did, but it hurt so bad and made me gag on the cloth stuffed deep into my throat.

"If y'all want in, yer gonna need a warrant. I know ya ain't got one" Hunter laughed. "I ain't got nothin' to hide, but I do respect my privacy".

"Sir" the unnamed man said. "We can't just barge in here like this, you know it's against all protocols".

They were outside my door. They were so close, and yet, all I wanted to do was fall asleep. I cried as my temple shut down. I cried as the drugs began fuelin' my body levels low. God I prayed fer a miracle I knew I wasn't gonna get.

My heart was barely beatin' by the time I was aware that I was comin' and goin' in and out of it. Their voices half awake and not at all. I started smilin', I found it all very funny. The two men I had the most intense feelin's fer, right next to each other.

"Mark my words" Colton hissed. "I know you've got everything to do with Millie's disappearance, and I will kill you myself when I get my answers".

I sobbed hysterically, wonderin' why he couldn't hear me. Rememberin' all of the promises we made in distant memories I knew I'd never get back. God, please let him hear me.

"You'll find they're quite closer than they appear" Hunter laughed.

Bodies shifted, there was even a slight dip in the light that cracked from beneath the door. Oh how I wanted someone to knock, tellin' me they were ready to take me home. That I did what I could, and it was enough.

"What did you just say?".

A loud knock did nothin' to me as a body fell onto my door fer support. I could picture it all very well. My door looked like a wall, there was no way someone could tell I was behind it. Hunter didn't fight back, and fer good reason. He knew he could take Colton to court fer invadin' his home and layin' his hands.

It sounded like Colton was bein' dragged away by the other officer. Hunter got up, must've been him that fell. They all walked down the stairs and I was deaf forever if I was gonna live another day after bein' so close.

Still, I questioned. Did they not see the candles? My flannel on the couch? Did they not see the plates on the dinin' table that fed two or three? God, did I not cry loud enough as they stood not even a foot away from me?

But he left.

With everythin' I ever had.

He left.

Me.

CHAPTER XII

It'd been a few weeks since I last heard Colton's voice. I wasn't doin' too well about it either. Hunter told me I hallucinated the whole thing, said somethin' about it bein' my pregnancy brain. I didn't believe him at first, but as hours turned into days and days into weeks, I was startin' to think he was right.

The police came by one night, I heard em' when I was *sleepin'* in Hunter's bed. He chained me up that night too, leavin' bruises on my ankles. So I know it actually happened. I could just barely hear em' like they were a whisper teasin' my ear.

They asked if Hunter wanted to press charges against Colton, but I think he said no. I wondered if he didn't cause then it would've drawn attention to him.

"We are all devastated with her disappearance" he said. *"Please make sure he's takin' care of himself".*

I pretended to be asleep when he came back up the stairs, knowin' well enough he'd hurt me fer eavesdroppin' so much. God it wasn't my fault, if he ain't want me hearin' so much, he should've kept me in that room he called mine.

He undid my chains when he came back, kissin' my ankles and tellin' me he was sorry, but it was cause of me that I couldn't be trusted. Everyday there was somethin' wrong and it was my fault fer it. Everyday I was blamed fer burnt food I never cooked, a mess I couldn't reach, and nauseatin' waves I couldn't control.

I sighed to myself as I put on my clothes fer the day; black long sleeve and a pair of jeans. I practically shared the room with Hunter now, usin' my designated spots fer my own things and the gifts he'd bring me. The sun poured in through the windows, illuminatin' everythin' clearly.

I walked towards the portal and placed a hand on its chillin' glass. My breath fogged it up a bit, but I simply wiped it away. It was beautiful outside. Though the cornfields were dyin', the trees in the far-off distance were comin' to life as different shades of orange, red, yellow, and green.

That was always my favorite part of autumn, the trees changin' their colors fer everyone to see no matter where they were at in life. I dropped my hand and replaced it with my forehead, silently whimperin' to myself that I might not get to go outside and enjoy the pumpkin scented breeze, apple cider donuts, or the coolin' winds.

I never would've thought my life would be like this. Kidnapped, livin' a life I couldn't escape cause I was too weak, and pregnant with my rapist's child. I didn't even know if I could even love the child, let alone raise it.

My heart started to quicken and a cold sweat broke out above my upper lip and forehead. What was I gonna do? How was I gonna teach this baby right from wrong when I couldn't even do that fer myself? How was I gonna act like the mother I had growin' up when the baby had no room to grow?

That's when it hit me, that baby was my way out. Surely Hunter would take me to the hospital in eight or nine months. Surely I could hold off until then and beg him to take me cause of the pain. He wouldn't be so cruel to let me birth at home alone.

But I was stupid.

Because he was cruel.

Because he was all sorts of messed up.

And I was too.

"June" a knock on the door brought me to my senses. "Come down stairs, my love. I have a surprise waitin' fer ya".

I stared back out that window and wondered how long it would take fer me to shatter it, build up the courage and jump out. I wondered forever how long it would take fer me to run past the endless rows of corn of all things, just to find someone willin' to listen and help me.

"June" he grazed my covered elbow. "Come with me".

His voice was soft and sweet, and if things were different, maybe I could've forced myself to love him. I prayed to God fer them thoughts to be burned away by the flames of hell because I knew they were sick.

I turned 'round and faced the man that claimed he loved me and would never hurt me, but my bruised skin and hollowed heart begged to differ. I replied yes and let him carry me away swiftly down the stairs and to the back door.

I was practically drained of all energy, light, and life when he looked at me. I gave him no response to his questionin' gaze, nor did I kiss him back when he pressed his lips to mine. A dark wave hit me instantly, and even if I were sane, I knew I wouldn't be surprised.

"Things will get better" he placed a hand on my stomach and another kiss to my lips.

I tried to smile, but I think it was just pity fer him so he wouldn't hurt me. I was programmed that way, tryin' to please him without even knowin' now that's what I was doin'.

He opened the back door and we stepped outside together on the wrap 'round porch. He told me to close my eyes and I did, because there was nothin' more I could do to retaliate. I let him guide me across the squeaky floorin', makin' sure to slide my feet a bit so they wouldn't trip and need his hold.

"Ya can open" he whispered to the top of my head.

I slowly opened my eyes and was taken back at what lied ahead. In the corner of the porch, there was a small area dedicated to me. Autumn's colors decorated a square table with dried leaves, a small banner with my new name, and a cake.

"Happy birthday, June".

"Happy birthday, Millie" the group said all at once.

"Thanks fer joinin' us" Abe placed a kiss on the top of my head.

Abilene removed her hands from my eyes and I about lost it. We were celebratin' my birth at her house since mama and I's was too small fer everyone, not that there was a whole lot of people to begin with.

They dedicated the livin' room as the main spot fer decorations, which consisted of colored balloons that floated to the ceilin', streamers, a happy birthday sign, and pictures of me, Abe, Colton, mama, Cheryl, and Virginia.

I was a softie at heart, tearin' up as I looked 'round the smilin' faces that wanted to celebrate my comin' down to earth. Abe and I never liked the idea of sayin' 'happy birthday', so we came up with 'comin' down to earth' as a replacement.

The night was filled with games, music, and adult watchin' once they got pretty into the drinks. Abe, Colton, and I made bets on who would pass out, throw up, or injure themselves first. I never betted on mama; she knew how to handle her liquor.

Usually, it was Virginia, Colton's mama. She'd pat her cheeks whenever the alcohol started settin' in, and she'd say how she wasn't feelin' anythin' yet, despite her rosy cheeks. I'd normally wait fer her to put her long thick and curly hair up in a bun before bettin', cause that's when I knew she was a gonner.

I never really liked celebratin' my birthdays, cause I often didn't feel special enough at the time. I wished everyone would come together and we could just celebrate as one. I didn't quite understand it myself.

However, that night was one of my most cherished memories I ever had. It was a warm blanket on a windy night that could shelter away my pains fer just another day.

By the end of the night, the adults left us, and my best friends and I were half asleep on the large sofa. We laid next to the fireplace, warmin' up in each other's heat and the fire's. Abilene was the first to fall asleep, always was, but I didn't mind.

Colton wrapped his arm 'round me and brought me in closer. Our bodies were practically smushed up against each other, yet I felt so far away from him. We talked our ears off until he kissed me and my thoughts fell silent.

I was the one to pull away, streamin' memories from a life I wanted to forget. I did that often, especially with Colton. He was the only one I wanted most, and yet, I couldn't even allow myself fer that to happen.

I was stuck, too trapped in the past to allow my muddy boots to come outta the mud and dry off fer once so I could walk straight. He asked if I was okay and I simply nodded that I was tired. He told me he didn't understand me, and I told him I didn't understand myself either.

"Talk to me" Colton whispered quiet so only I could hear. "Tell me what's on your mind".

"Another time" I rest my head on his chest as bold as I was and my body quickly fell asleep. I apologized to him fer bein' wishy washy. I apologized fer leadin' him on, lettin' him get close, only to push him even further away.

But I never said it out loud.

"I didn't mean to make ya cry".

My hands quickly wiped away the tears that turned cold on my skin. I was alone, forgotten, and I was goin' to die in a prison made of false light. Knowin' it was my birthday meant I'd spent almost a year with Hunter.

It meant my friends and family were startin' to move on, never knowin' what happened to me. Never knowin' that I was probably much closer than we all thought.

So, I stared at the small corner meant to celebrate my life, even though I had never felt more dead in my entire existence. Never had I felt so empty, discarded, and laid to waste. Never had I wanted to die so much than in that moment.

I smiled at myself; Hunter joined in fer reasons he knew nothin' about. I was just then realizin' that I could handle the pain, the rape, and everythin' that came with Hunter's obsession. Everythin' but the loneliness, because that's exactly what I was.

Even with a baby inside of me, I was completely and utterly alone.

"How old am I?" I looked at him with teary eyes.

"What do ya mean?" he smiled a laugh. "Ya don't know?".

I shook my head and he sat me down on the swingin' bench to the left of the door we'd just entered. He kissed the top of my head, smoothed out my hair, and walked towards the cake. When he came back, a single burnin' candle laid on top.

"Make a wish" he crouched to my height.

The candlelight danced off his skin in hues of orange and yellow, morphin' his face into some kind of person I knew more than the actual one in front of me. Make a wish? I frowned and bit my lower lip, hopin' anythin' could distract me from what I really wanted.

I wish you were dead.

I wish I was with mama.

I wish I was with Colton.

He seemed annoyed with my unspoken wishes, my unwillingness to actually commit to the unsaid timeframe he setup fer me. I could only pick one with the amount of life I had left in me. I could only choose one.

I wish you were dead.

"Well?" he raised a brow. "Was it a good one?".

"I hope so".

He brought his lips to mine and I let him, almost forgettin' that I didn't like it, that I did it only fer him. He walked the cake back to the table and I watched with delicate eyes as he cut two slices for us. I thanked him when he handed me the dessert.

The sweet and sugary food kissed my lips and my eyes opened wide. It was the same recipe as the one mama used to make. It wasn't just the taste, consistency, or the smell. Warm vanilla danced on my tongue, while sweet almond extract bathed in the cream cheese frostin'.

Decorated in blackberries, strawberries, blueberries, and a curve to the pippin', everythin' about this cake had mama written all over it. Like she had made it herself.

I looked at Hunter, he was watchin' me cautiously. He smirked and forked the rest of his half down when he realized I figured it out that mama had made this cake.

"How?" I whispered.

"How what, June? Yer gonna need to clarify" he smiled, takin' my empty plate from me and settin' it aside.

"How did you get this?".

"I made it".

"Hunter" I grabbed onto his arm, shocked by my own disobedience. "Please".

"Yer mama made it" he sighed. "She's been makin' these cakes all week to celebrate yer birthday. Everyone in town practically got one".

Mama was goin' crazy.

"Tell her I'm okay" I held onto him tighter. "Tell her I'm okay, Hunter".

I looked back and forth from Hunter to the porch stairs, just wonderin' if I was fast enough to make a break fer it. Hopin' that I was good enough to get half way and cry fer help prayin' someone would hear me if I tried hard enough.

"There's a way fer ya to see her" he held onto my inner thigh with his cold hands.

"How?" I spoke too fast fer my own good.

He said nothin' and I asked again, it was like some sick torturin' plan of his to destroy me inside and out. God if it wasn't physical, he knew how to play the strings of my heart as an orchestrator would his orchestra.

"Ya just gotta be a good girl and I'll loosen up the reigns" he grabbed my hand and led me down the stairs. "Ever since comin' here, ya changed, been distant, sendin' off mixed signals. I dunno what to do with ya sometimes cause I feel you'll never change".

Delusional. He's delusional in every way possible. I tiptoed behind him down the stairs and onto the dirt path leadin' into the cornfields.

My shoes crunched on crisp leaves from trees that didn't want their organic décor to stay home. I took a deep breath in and my stomach tightened in the cold air.

"I'm sorry" I lied.

"That's just it" he paused, holdin' onto my arm tightly. "I don't think ya are. You've done nothin' but make life harder fer me. I wouldn't change it fer the world, but I hoped ya would've come around to me by now".

"I don't understand" I whispered to the ground. "I- I do like you, a lot".

He was goin' to kill me.

Say what he wants to hear, Millie.

"Don't play the fool, June" his fingers were piercin' through my forearm as he dragged me inside the field of corn. "I know this ain't the life ya pictured, but can't ya just accept it? Why do ya need other people when ya got me?".

"You're right" I paused and he stopped too. "I'm sorry. You've done a lot fer me and I haven't shown you any gratitude. We're havin' a baby together now; shouldn't that mean somethin' from God?".

He smiled, placin' a hand behind my neck and up halfway my head. His fingers curled my hair 'round 'em and he lifted my eyes up to his. He looked back and forth in them like there was an unspoken word between us.

"Marry me?" he kissed my lips hard.

I couldn't respond. Say no. Say no. Say no. I couldn't respond to anythin' cause I couldn't breathe. He pulled me into a small clearin' that had a red blanket on the ground and cushioned pillows 'round the sides.

Though the sun was set high in the cold world above us, my surroundins' were darkened too much. I thought of the time he first took me into the fields when we were children and my heart sped. He had his way with me over and over, until the sight of me wasn't enough.

He needed me.

So he took me.

"Marry me, June" he said again.

"Will you take me to my mama if I do?" I stupidly asked aloud.

He broke our connection, lettin' me catch my breath in the process. His hand fell slowly from my face and down to his side, like I was made of fire and he couldn't handle the burn any longer. There was hurt in his eyes, tremble in his lips, and anger in his soul that made me back up.

"Is that all ya care about? Seein' yer mama?" he shouted. "I'm right here in front of ya. Isn't that enough? Aren't I enough?".

"Hunter, I-I'm so-".

He raised his fist and cracked my nose, sendin' me to the earth's floor. He told me I was ungrateful, that I cared too much fer my past and too little fer him. I tried tellin' him I didn't mean it how I said. I tried tellin' him I'd be good, that I wouldn't trouble him no more.

"I've told ya before so there's no point in tellin' ya again of all the sacrifices I have to make to keep ya happy. So why can't ya just love me how I love ya".

He picked up his foot and kicked me in the ribs, sendin' me deep into the earth. I was cryin' by the time I even realized it. He told me to shut up, again and again. With every kick, his foot dug deeper and deeper into my stomach.

My lips parted slightly as I gasped fer air, needin' more every time I opened my mouth. I wasn't gonna die this time, but I think that scared me most. At least with the promise of death, I knew I wasn't gonna remember much in the afterlife.

Sharp pains spread like wildfire in my stomach. I think I screamed fer it, the baby. It tried crawlin' outta my mouth, but my body wasn't gonna let it out so easily. It pulled my head back and shot electric pulses behind my eyes.

I knew I was gonna live this time 'round. He was just gonna beat me real bad, until I caved in, passed out, reopened wounds he thought would kill me.

"Marry me, June" he crouched down to lift my head.

I tried to whisper 'yes' cause I knew even sayin' that wouldn't legally do nothin' fer us. If he ever brought me somewhere, I'd be found within an instant.

And he knew that.

Which is how I knew I was never leavin' this house.

Which is how he knew he could never have the life he wanted with me.

He told me I was too quiet, that no one was gonna come fer me. I was good fer dead in their eyes. I was good enough fer dead in my own eyes too. He punched me in the face, bustin' my nose open again, bustin' my lip, crackin' a back tooth, and he even got on top to strangle me.

"Stop" I raised my arm with a whisper on my lips.

I was goin' in and out of consciousness, tryin' to get him to stop killin' me before resurrections the next day. He stood straight, backin' up just a few paces fer me to compose myself. I could hardly see. I could hardly breathe.

He bent near my head and grabbed onto my growin' hair, pullin' me across the earth's floor. There was a lot of stuff he was sayin' about me, a lot of stuff he was sayin' to me. All I could focus on was them small rocks tearin' open my shirt, scratchin' my skin deep.

He threw my body onto the red blanket and had his way in between. Over and over, he did everythin' he wanted to do with me. There was no point in sayin' 'no'. There was no point in cryin' again. There was no point fer nothin'.

I'm sorry, but I am like a seesaw. Teeter-totterin' like I actually have a choice in the way my mind works.

Can I not have pity fer even myself?

I woke up that night chained to his bed, dressed in small and pink satin pajamas. I couldn't move my head or my eyes because they burned, scratchin' every bit of me like nails on a chalkboard each time I moved.

I looked 'round with swollen and painfully sharp eyes before sittin' up. I might've screamed a little too when my body straightened. I grabbed onto the sides of my head, slippin' my fingers to my neck. My eyes shot open wide and I viciously played with the freshly cut ends of my hair.

I wondered if he dyed it again, or if it was only cut just below my jaw. It didn't matter to me because I knew I had more important wounds to address. My eyes, nose, the back of my head, and even my back were completely ripped apart. They were pulsatin' and whimperin' my body like I survived hell.

A sudden and sharp ache moved throughout my stomach and I grabbed onto the lower part, hopin' to alleviate some of the pain. Nothin' worked and I sobbed like I had lost myself again.

They were the worst cramps of my life. They made me nauseous, sat me straight, and blinded my eyes so I couldn't see reality.

I moved 'round a bit and felt somethin' warm between my legs. I placed two fingers below and brought them back up, now smellin' like iron. I couldn't see much, but I knew they were wet. I let go again to stain my pajamas with the blood I knew was now on my fingers.

My throat dropped deep into my stomach and I sobbed louder to myself, bringin' up a pillow to mask the noise. I didn't know if I was cryin' fer relief or to mourn the life that died inside of me because I wasn't strong enough.

I wondered if I should've called fer Hunter. It was his loss too cause I was havin' a miscarriage. Thoughts rambled and raced through my mind about what I should do. I couldn't tell him about it, he would blame me fer it.

And who the hell was I to even owe him a say in the rape he took part in. He'd say I wasn't eatin' enough, that I purposefully killed it. He would've never admitted that it was him. That when he kicked me, punched me, tore me open to have his fill, he could've done it.

Still, there was one thing I knew fer sure. Somethin' I never wanted to do again after the first time and so soon. Somethin' I knew would save my life and kill me both at the same time fer whatever heinous crimes, yet this way was easier.

I needed to get pregnant again.

Cause if not.

He was gonna kill me fer it.

And I knew I needed to survive.

CHAPTER XIII

About a week passed since Hunter beat my baby outta me. I often think it was a girl and her name was Max. She looked more like Hunter than she did me, and I wondered if I would've hated her fer it. Even if someone saved our lives, I pondered if I'd blame her fer whatever problems.

But I couldn't.

Cause she saved me.

Hunter hadn't come in the room much, wasn't even sleepin' with me. I wore the same pink satin pajamas I'd stained with blood and the same wounds that needed adressin'. He took my chains off last night when I was sleepin', I knew he was startin' to feel bad about everythin'.

Or maybe he thought my punishment was over.

I laid in bed depressed, exponentially exhausted, and feelin' like my world was completely cavin' in. I felt empty, my stomach was empty. There was no life in there or my entire body. I ain't have anythin' worth livin' fer.

And yet, somethin' told me to keep goin'.

I pretended to be asleep when Hunter came in, leavin' me my breakfast on a small table in the left corner of the room. He made that fer me after the first time he locked me in here. Said somethin' about him not wantin' me eatin' on the bed or floor.

He sighed, and though my eyes were closed, I could've felt his dauntin' stare from ten thousand miles away. He whispered under his breath that I was killin' myself to torture him by not eatin' last night's dinner.

It was only partially true.

I didn't eat his food cause I knew it was wrong of me to do. I knew it would send him the signal that everythin' was fine, when in fact, I couldn't even convince myself a penny near it was. He stomped his feet as he left, yet shut the door as if it were the baby he thought we still had.

"I'll kill ya if I find ya haven't moved a single inch" he whispered through the crack of the door. "It ain't good fer ya, naw is it fer our baby".

My eyes closed tighter and I gripped harder onto the blankets I laid decayin' underneath. I counted his steps patiently, waitin' fer him to reach the bottom of the stairs before I couldn't hear no more.

He was cynical.

And so was I.

My stomach growled immediately once he left and I knew I should've held off as long as I could, but the body wants what the body needs. Unfortunately, God made it so I was what Hunter strangely needed. I let go of the white knuckles I had grippin' onto the blankets and I pushed my achin' body up.

My back, elbows, wrists, and even my knees cracked as I straightened up and rest my back against the brown leather headboard. God I was livin' it. I ripped the sheets off my body and set my feet on the warm rug underneath me.

With an arm supportin' each of my sides, I took three deep breaths and lifted myself up. I took not even one step before fallin' to the ground. The inside of my thighs was hurtin' terribly, and my head decided to jump ship the moment I set sail and stood.

I hoped my body didn't make a loud sound hittin' the floor as it did. I didn't want him comin' back up, seein' all the blood and blamin' me fer ruinin' his sheets. Just as I thought it, the front door slammed shut, tellin' me he wasn't gonna be back fer hours.

I got my body to sit upright again, this time usin' the bedframe fer support. Counted to three just as I did before with my breath and I clawed my way up. My head started spinnin' and I dropped my elbows onto the mattress.

Luckily fer me, the bedframe held the actual mattress itself to my hips. I stayed with my legs stretched out straight and my dropped elbows fer a minute or so before tellin' myself it was time to move on. It was all to distract myself from the food on the table.

My stomach demanded this time it got fed, and I swore children's substitutes under my breath. I propped my head up and looked 'round the room, gluin' my eyes to the small linen closet in the corner. I wobbled my way over, holdin' onto everythin' and anythin' I could to get to the other side.

He designed this room perfectly, it had eveythin' I needed so I wouldn't have to leave. From the small table in the corner, to my dressers, the bed, the bathroom, the small linen closet, and even the remote TV he just put in there. The only thing missin' without him there was food.

Everythin' was startin' to look the same to me. Everythin' was blendin' into one. God I was goin' crazy from bein' locked up in this darn room fer so long. I tore open the lengthy wooden doors to the linen closet and I began rippin' everythin' out.

Towels, sheets, soaps, toilet paper, and so much more. I tossed and ripped apart that entire closet and turned towards the room to do the same. I was huffin' and puffin' by the time my body completely exhausted itself and I fell back to the floor.

I wiped away tears of frustration and my eyes opened wide. There was a cold shiver to my face when I touched it. I knew it was badly beaten, but this was from somethin' else. I looked at my hands, gaspin' when I saw the ring on my left hand.

It was silver all 'round, with a small diamond cut to the shape of an almond, encased by twelve smaller ones. I didn't remember him puttin' it on my hand, signifyin' eternity with him. He asked me to marry him, I said yes, still it wasn't good enough, and he beat me.

My eyes closed, my body died, and I had no memories of everythin' I did of what I was doin, had done, and still had left to do. I just remember screamin', tellin' everyone that had ever failed me to screw off. Tellin' myself I was the worst of them all.

I knew I was movin' 'round, pickin' up heavy stuff, and droppin' it down. I couldn't control the stir-crazed energy inside of me even if I wanted to. I was too far long gone fer anythin' to fix me. So I left it overtake me.

My eyes were stained red, heart heavy, and lips remainin' silent. My skin was hot, boilin' like an inferno. God give me the strength cause I wanted him to pay for what he'd done.

I was playin' with the ends of my new hair by the time I came back to my senses, realizin' what I had done to the room. It was fine fer me, I couldn't recollect what happened. I was in the bathroom already, starin' at the girl in the mirror.

She was unrecognizable, too dirty.

I stripped myself naked and threw the pajamas I'd been wearin' fer the past week into the trash. It wasn't a salute to Hunter, more so because I would never wear those again. I stepped onto the white tiled floor in the large glass encompassed shower and I let the hot water burn my skin cold.

It took a few seconds fer the dried blood to loosen and fall in chunks down my body. I watched each piece slowly trickle down my skin, fall onto the floor, and I'd kick it towards the drain in the middle of the shower fer it to flow down.

I wished it was that easy fer me.

I stayed in the shower until the water turned cold and my skin could no longer tolerate the blue/red turnin' tint. I walked out naked, not carin' about how badly my body was shakin', and I dressed myself in Hunter's large green robe.

I used my hand to wipe away the dispersin' fog from the mirror and I placed small fingers on the girl starin' back. Before she was unrecognizable, and now, it was still the same. I didn't know who she was. Her hair was back to her natural color of dark brown, but it was cut short again, below her jaw and above her shoulders.

My eyes were blue/green underneath, my bottom lip was split in the right corner, my nose had a deep green bruise accompanied by a short laceration that went over the bridge. I was surprised how my body could heal so fast, or maybe I never got hurt to the extent I thought I actually did.

I was a mess.

So was Hunter's room.

I thought just once I could be the problem, that I could destroy and not create. As usual, I was wrong. I flipped the TV onto the news station and I turned down the volume so I could hear if Hunter had come back early or not.

I started with the bedsheets, rippin' them off and washin' out the blood as much as I could with the moveable shower head. Just as I thought, it was pretty much stained all over. I took out some of the clothes from the laundry hamper and threw the sheets in the middle just to make sure he wouldn't notice the stains.

I grabbed fresh sheets from the floor and redressed the bed. My arms ached, as did my legs, but I knew I had to restore the room to the best I could before he got back. I smoothed out the last of the thick navy-blue sheets and began foldin' the others I dismantled.

Whispers from the TV behind urged me to look at it's screen. They were talkin' about the man in the woods that Hutner killed, of course they knew nothin' about it. My body sat upright when they mentioned findin' my blood.

"Lost cause" I told them. "There's no use".

They tried makin' assumptions about what happened to me, I guess I was becomin' pretty famous. Everyone had somethin' to say about me, whether they thought I was dead or not. I guess they were right in some kind of way, I was dead. I died the moment he took me and was reborn as somethin' else.

I was gonna have to figure out whoever *she* was.

But not here, no. There were too many crazed voices walkin' 'round my head to let myself go off and explore my mind. What?

I didn't really like watchin' my case on TV anymore, maybe it was programmed into me to be like that or somethin'. I just couldn't stand watchin' the police fail me time after time. I couldn't stand them thinkin' they got some kind of lead when I was just a few miles away from them.

Sometimes I think how I don't want 'em to find me in his home. I wonder if they'd look at the wooden doors and wonder why I didn't knock them down, why I couldn't pick the locks, break free from the metal barred windows.

I wasn't strong enough.

The soft voice of a man I once knew carried me to the screen and sat my body down on the floor like I was a kid watchin' cartoons before school. His sandy brown hair was longer now, tucked behind his ears, and his full lips pinched into worry lines I wanted to reassure were fer nothin'.

"Survive" his amber eyes looked straight into the camera. "All you've gotta do is survive, Millie. Just another night".

Just one more.

My stomach growled and I left my eyes from his fer just a moment to stare at the food Hunter made me fer me in the mornin'. When I came back, he was gone, the station had moved on to another case of home burglary that was increasin' in the bigger cities.

I grabbed the remote and pointed it at the TV, shuttin' it off so I could enjoy whatever silence this home offered me. My stomach wouldn't budge with its continuous disturbances and my headache didn't make it any better.

I gave in.

I practically knocked over the table as I sat and scarfed down the food. It was delicious, or maybe I was just starvin' myself so much that everythin' tasted good to me. Survive, survive, survive. I smiled as I took a bite into the warm toast.

I was goin' crazy.

Cause I kept seein' Colton's ghost.

When he wasn't ever there.

I spent the rest of the day cleanin' the mess I made, makin' sure every inch of that room was clean fer when he got back. He'd have no excuses to hit me since I had obviously been movin' 'round, but I still thought about his imperfect promises.

He was the record that played over and over because it was broken, and I was just a mere bystander, forced to listen to the intoxicatin'ly annoyin' track. All day I spent waitin' in that room fer him, wonderin' whether or not he was gonna come.

When everythin' was finished, the sun was already comin' down and I was starvin'. I hadn't much to do, my books were in the other room only Hunter and I knew about, and he wasn't here to bring me any meals.

I stopped thinkin' about food, knowin' it just made things worse. I focused more on the room that Colton and his colleague passed- if that even was a real memory.

I had no scars, no marks on my body to show that everythin' that happened actually did happen that day. That's how I told myself what was real or not, if I had any scars on my body to show fer it. I brushed my fingers gently over my arms, goin' even softer when I hit certain scars.

There was a deep one on my left arm, I almost smiled just rememberin' how I got it.

"June" Hunter yelled from downstairs.

I had no chains, no restraints holdin' me back from wanderin' round the house. Yet, I stayed in his room the entire time. He was makin' chicken and potatoes fer dinner, even told me he'd been learnin' how to make a cranberry pie.

I think he wasn't a bad person, just lonely.

"I'll be down soon" I called to him.

I quickly dried off my body and changed into a dark green nightgown. It was lowcut, sinched at the waist, and hugged every one of my curves. I was beyond uncomfortable in the soft fabric, but there wasn't much I could do about it.

I was tryin' to get him to trust me, to show him I was worthy of keepin' round and not killin'. I walked downstairs and he began clappin', callin' himself the luckiest man on the planet.

I wanted to vomit.

I pretended I liked it.

Hunter scooped me into a hug and practically carried me to my seat at the table. I watched him walk away and come back with our plates in hand. He set his down first and then mine, only to place a kiss on the top of my head.

"I hope ya like it, my love".

He sat down and watched as I took my first bite. As much as I hated to admit it, I enjoyed it a lot. He was a really good cook; everyone liked his food.

I tried to imagine a life where he wasn't deranged, and I wondered if I would ever go fer someone like him. He wasn't attractive to me, but his cookin' was good, he had a stable job, and he made good money doin' it too.

"What's wrong?" he whispered, grabbin' onto my hand across the candlelit table.

"Nothin' at all" I pitied him a smile.

He grunted like he was annoyed, and before I had the time to look up at him, there was a hot searin' pain comin' from my arm. I followed his free hand just below my elbow and high above my wrist.

He stabbed me.

He actually stabbed me.

I looked back and forth between him and the knife protrudin' from my forearm, wonderin' what I did wrong.

"Ya will tell me what's on yer mind when I ask" he gripped onto the handle and ripped the knife upwards.

My breathin' fastened and my head became light. My once hazel eyes rolled to the back of my head, turnin' white, and my head fell back with the rest of my body.

He was a keeper, that's fer sure. I joked to myself, unamused with the dark and twisted humor I decided to laugh about.

Time moved by so slow, it felt like I was drugged again. I was already dressed fer bed, wearin' blue plaid pajama pants and a large black shirt, both belongin' to Hunter. If I was gonna be told off fer not doin' anythin', wearin' his clothes was best proof to show I had done somethin'.

I thought to stay awake and wait fer him, but the clock read almost midnight. I guessed today was a Friday or Saturday and he was out drinkin' with the boys. Those were always my favorite nights outta the week.

I had more time fer myself, and in most cases, Hunter was too drunk to make it up the stairs fer bed. He'd come in the mornin' all angry, but usually he'd scurry off into the shower to make it in time fer work. I wished everyday was like a Friday or Saturday.

I closed the curtains and said my nightly prayers, though I found no point in really doin' them no more. I had nothin' to pray about, and I even sounded like the broken record and not Hunter as I continued to pray fer someone to save me.

Anyone.

"Amen" I whispered to no one, not even God.

I crawled in bed and let the heavy sheets hold my decayin' corpse down firm. I was just a floatin' head if anyone were to actually see me. I counted sheep in my head, yet I couldn't fall asleep. I guess I hadn't done much to deserve sleep.

The clock read thirty past midnight as it shined white numbers on Hunter's side of the room. I'd been tryin' to fall asleep fer too long it felt like a job I'd never get paid fer. It was just another thing to add to my list of things I wasn't able to do.

I couldn't even talk to the one man I needed to impress most without showin' how I felt on the inside. I was a failure, completely and utterly, an unsuccessful failure to myself and others. They said be strong, but my courage was never born with me. They said to be a lot of things I couldn't.

But what if I tried?

What more did I have to lose if not fer my life? I had already killed my baby's chance at livin', what couldn't I do?

I flipped the sheets off me and I ran to the door, wantin' to open that handle so badly. My body was unusually sprung to life with a force I needed to have from the very beginnin'. I wasn't sure where it came from, or what it wanted with me.

All I knew was that I had to try.

Just as I reached fer the handle, it wiggled from the other side.

Run.

I quickly ran to the bed and jumped under its sheets before his head popped through, and then his body. I didn't hear him come home; I didn't hear nothin'. No truck muffler, no loud keys danglin' about, nothin'.

"June" Hunter whispered.

I didn't answer and he told me he heard me runnin' away from him. Keys clattered in his hands and he even dropped them before pickin' them up again. He swore loudly, frustrated with how many there were and how many he had to keep cause of me.

"Stand up" I did as he said.

I flattened the sheets as if no one had ever slept in them and we approached each other, meetin' just perfectly between the bed and door. Though I could hardly see him, I knew he was a mess. He wreaked of alcohol and fried foods.

He grabbed onto both my shoulders and squeezed hard on 'em before kickin' off his boots. There was somethin' off, somethin' strange about the way he was actin'. He asked why I was by the door, if I was tryin' to get out and leave him.

I told him everythin' was okay and that I wouldn't ever think about leavin' him, that that part of me was over and gone. Hunter forced a kiss on my lips and lifted the bottom of my shirt up.

"Why ya wearin' my clothes, June" he placed a liquor infused and sloppy kiss on my forehead.

"I missed you, that's all" I kissed him back.

"Ya don't like what I bought ya?" his voice changed, my heart sank, I couldn't breathe. "Tell me ya love me, won't ya?".

Even if I meant it, even if I wanted to, I couldn't. His hands wrapped 'round my throat, tightenin' with each and every passin' second I couldn't account fer. We fell to the ground together, and fer a moment, he let go to roll on top of me.

"Hunter" I called out his name. "I love you".

I could just barely see a smile on his lips with the dim light comin' through the blinds of the windows. The moon wasn't full, but it also wasn't entirely gone as well.

He let go with one hand and the other was firm, glued to my skin. He told me I was lyin' with a sluggish lisp as he used his free hand to rip the pants right off of me.

"I don't want ya wearin' my stuff, June" he let go of my neck to use both hands to tear open the shirt. "It's harder to get to ya that way".

I told him I wouldn't, that we should talk things out. I told him a bunch of different lies to get him to stop, even told him it'd hurt the baby if he did this to me.

"I know that baby is dead" he used an open hand to smack me. "Ya killed it last week".

"It wasn't me" I swore.

"Then who was it, June? Was it me?".

I didn't have time to respond, cause he was draggin' me to the bed. Said he wanted me on the floor, but he'd show me forgiveness. I cried when he closed his fist around the hair on the back of my head and tilted my head up.

He spit in my mouth; told me I was a liar and that he was gonna kill me. The more I cried, the harder he pushed fer somethin' he knew I hated. He grabbed a paddle from the side of his bed and hit me in the thighs with it, then the face.

My head spun, I couldn't feel my toes or fingers, there was nerve damage. He laid me on the bed and sprawled out my body, everythin' was cold, even him. My eyes rolled to the back of my head and my thoughts left me completely.

I was fallin' in and out of consciousness, only hearin' his heavy breathin' as he worked himself in and out of me. He punched my stomach and fumbled with somethin' in the pockets of the pants he still had on.

His phone fell outta his pocket when he grabbed whatever it was he was fumblin' fer. I heard it hit the ground and bounce three times before settlin' just a tad under the bed on my side. I had to wait, take my time, and stay calm.

Somethin' clicked into place and he ran the dull side across my face, his pocket knife. He told me I'd been bad recently, that everythin' he'd done was fer nothin'. I truly thought I was gonna die. The blade dug deep into my shoulder and I finally felt warmth before it left too quickly.

Thinkin' it was somethin' I liked, he ran the knife across my arms, stomach, and legs before throwin' it to his side of the bed. I didn't think he stabbed deep enough to kill me from blood loss, but as the minutes carried on, I wished it would've.

He grabbed onto my open jaw, stickin' three fingers inside to hold onto my teeth fer support as he raped me. I couldn't even bite down, his force was too strong. His pace quickened until we both couldn't breathe and he finished inside of me, tellin' me it wasn't gonna do nothin' anyway.

He fell to my side and grabbed onto my body, curlin' me up into a little ball. He grabbed a fist of my hair, facin' my back, and he moved around my head while laughin'. Still, I knew somethin' wasn't right. He was gettin' riskier, and I didn't do nothin' fer him to revert.

"I'm goin' to kill ya tomorrow" he whispered in my ear with a hand around my throat.

My stomach dropped and I pinched my eyes tightly. Its strange how you can still cry when your eyes are closed, strange you can die while still bein' alive.

I waited fer what seemed like hours fer him to fall asleep behind me. I always knew when he did cause his grasp would loosen, sometimes he'd even turn completely 'round and face the bathroom. That's exactly what happened.

I carefully turned 'round myself and looked at him. He was disgustin' and vile, dick outta his zipper and sprawled out like he was worth somethin'. It was easier facin' the way

I was layin', even harder to get off the bed without him noticin'.

I rolled my entire body until I met the bed's edge, puttin' one foot down and then the other. I counted thirty-five seconds fer how long it took me to stand from the bed to make sure it wouldn't creak or nothin'.

Hunter tossed an arm my way and I quickly reacted by thowin' a pillow under, hopin' he'd think it was me. I watched him shuffle, play with himself a little, and go back to sleepin' deeply before I ducked under his view and searched fer his phone.

My hands fumbled in the dark, quietly pattin' the rug fer any indication of his phone. I crawled until I was practically underneath the bed. My hopes were lowerin' with each failed attempt I had at findin' the thing.

I had a savin' grace right in front of me, yet I couldn't see where it was. I thought about givin' up, thought about tossin' aside all hopes I had. I stood up and walked quietly back to the bed, not realizin' how far I'd actually gone from it.

Just as I placed a hand on the navy-blue sheets, a buzz came from below my feet. Quite precisely, directly underneath my left foot. I quickly dropped with my heart and grabbed the device between my hands, tearin' up before I even done anythin'.

The blindin' screen showed someone named Josh texted him. I turned down the brightness of his phone by swipin' down and I quickly remembered to hit do not disturb. I never owned a fancy touchscreen Hunter's had, but Abilene had a very similar one, and I learned what I could from her on how to use it.

I gave a moment to thank her, Abilene. I told no one but my own thoughts that were becomin' too hopeful too quickly. I should've known better than to think it was gonna be easy.

It didn't matter that Hunter had a password protected phone, all I had to do was swipe up and hit the emergency button. I looked 'round the room from my view on the floor, searchin' fer some place to make the call.

I shuffled on my hands and knees, breath increasin' fer the better, life comin' back into my body, and my soul tellin' me to keep goin'. I headed fer the bathroom, stayin' low to the ground so not even Hunter could see my shadow.

I passed the bedroom door and a breeze of cool air chilled my skin. I forgot I was completely naked. Luckily fer me, the hamper was right next to the door. I grabbed the first thing my hands touched; a manly scented grey sweater and the bottoms of my bloodied pink satin pajama shorts.

I quickly changed into the clothes, lookin' back every couple seconds or so to make sure Hunter hadn't woken up, that he wasn't starin' at me from above, just waitin' to kick or pounce on me. He was out, drunken past his limit of control.

Just as I was about to finish crawlin' to the bathroom, the cold breeze creaked the door. My head snapped in its direction and I saw a dim light from downstairs crackin' from underneath. I tried not to lose myself in a glory I had yet to sing.

He didn't close the door.

He forgot.

I have a chance.

I sat on my lap as I delicately placed both hands on the door. It creaked incredibly loud, but I hoped Hunter's snorin' masked it more. I crawled on my hands and knees when enough room presented itself, and I quickly closed it as quietly as I could.

Time ain't even move slow, it was pausin' fer me to catch my breath and then to loose it. God give me sane thoughts cause I thought I was still asleep, dreamin' a nightmare that was soon to come.

I stood lookin' down at the stairs, and the Lord told me to turn 'round. I did as he said and turned back towards the door, noticin' I could lock it from the outside.

Just as I did, it clicked, and Hunter's snorin' stopped with it. My heart told me to run after droppin' outta my chest, and so I did. I tried not fumblin' down the stairs, but I knew he was awake anyway.

I pulled out the phone as I pushed through the pain in my legs and abdomen, and I dialed the only number I knew I needed.

"911 what's your emergency?" she asked.

I almost dropped to the floor I was so exhausted. I thought I was goin' crazy, and now, I finally had someone to confirm or deny. I couldn't even decipher if they were talkin' to me or not. I didn't care because this was the closest I ever got to escapin'.

"Hello?" I whispered while runnin' to the front door. "My name is Millie Maye and I've been kidnapped".

There was a pause on her end and I repeated my statement, just barely bein' able to hold in my tears. The door's handle wouldn't budge, it was locked with different bolts painted in all different colors.

"Do you know where you're located?" she asked.

Hunter was bangin' on the bedroom door upstairs. He was mad, and I knew I wasn't gonna survive if he got out. I looked 'round the room fer anythin' to tell me the address, but I had no business to give em' a straight answer.

Each knock, every holler, my body jumped, twitched, screamed, and cried out.

"Don't do anythin' stupid, June" he screamed. "June!".

He told me he loved me, that I was bein' irrational. He kept repeatin' that dang name over and over. My back hit the wall, I knocked off a frame, and glass shattered everywhere. I slid down the empty wall and sat on the floor with my knees to my chest.

"Make it stop" I whispered "Please make it stop".

I covered my ears with my bleedin' hands, not realizin' one of 'em had been clutchin' onto some broken glass from the frame.

"Do you know where you're located, Millie?" she asked again.

"June!" Hunter yelled.

It sounded like he was breakin' down the door. Wood splintered off itself, some hittin' the wall across from it, some fallin' down the stairs.

I wasn't gonna survive this time.

Survive. Survive. Survive. Colton said to the camera, lookin' right at me.

"No" I whimpered, jaw tremblin' and all. "Hunter Davis- please hurry".

I could hardly breathe; he was smashin' through the bedroom door even harder. He was goin' so hard at it he was makin' things on the first-floor shake. I thought it could've been mistaken fer an earthquake.

"Hunter Davis is there with you?".

"He's gonna kill me" I cried hysterically. "We're surrounded by corn fields. He knows I don't like em' too".

She asked if I was okay, if he was gonna hurt me, and I told her he already had. I told her he was gonna kill me soon, especially now that I called. I asked her to be fast, to hurry, but they had no address to go off of.

I tried describin' everythin' the best I could, but I hadn't been out many times, and when I did, he always drugged me up or took me out the back way. So I sat there, defeated by the front door, cryin' to the operator and askin' her to tell my mama I tried.

I heard mama's voice tellin' me it wasn't my time. She wrapped me in her arms and carried me outta that house. I was tired, so tired, and I just wanted to sleep. I was a child again, layin' in her arms as she hummed me to sleep. Just before I dosed, I looked behind her and saw the house that kept me bonded in blood.

"There's three steps leadin' from the wrap 'round porch to the ground. I think the house is red, dark red".

Remember, remember, I told myself as I scrunched my brows together.

"There's numbers on the outside walls too. I think 8-7-2- I'm not sure. There's cornfields around us. There's corn everywhere, and I can never see past it" I cried. "That's all I know".

I came back to my senses, surprised by my divinely times remembrance.

"We're going to get-" the angel's tongue was cut off by the devil.

"June? What are ya doin?".

CHAPTER XIV

A loud and sharp pain rang through my ears and my vision started mushin', like dirt on a rainy day. He was just a grey shadow standin' in front of me, voice mufflin' and all. He tore the phone from my hand, first havin' to pry my fingers off.

I opened my mouth to speak, to say I was sorry, but they fumbled because they knew I'd be lyin', and mama always told me that liars always got caught. He threw his phone on the ground and grabbed the dinin' chair to break it.

My future, my small friend in the box was now shattered into a million pieces, takin' my freedom with em'. My mouth dropped, my hands and elbows hit the floor. My skin turned hot, bleedin' out I assumed from only God knows what, but I was not gonna die without fulfillin' mama's wish.

Fight.

I wasn't audible as I screamed, pushin' off my arms and standin' on my feet. I still couldn't see all that well, my head was throbbin', my ears rang, and I was sure blood was comin' outta my mouth. I pressed my hands firmly onto his chest and pushed as pathetically as I could.

My hands were slippery, he stepped back and knocked into the dinin' table. I think he was playin' with me like I was some mouse in his traps. I think he was hittin' me too, but I couldn't see past the point from which I was almost freed.

"What more do you want?" I clawed at his face. "What more can you take from me?".

He grabbed onto my wrists and pushed me back onto the wall, pinnin' my hands above my head. He said my falsified name and told me to look up. I stared into his eyes until my own unearthed themselves and I could see him well under the light of my anger.

"Look what ya done to yourself" he painfully plucked a thick shard of glass outta my palm. "Ya hurt yerself".

My body wanted to fight, it wanted me to keep goin', to stay alive. I guess that much was true since I ain't even notice the long dagger I picked up from the ground to kill him with. He dropped an arm, holdin' both of mine with one of his.

"You hurt me too" I followed his hand as it wiped the deep cut I etched under his eye and over his nose.

I smiled, I was crazy fer laughin' too. It was the first time I ever hurt him like that. He didn't find me amusin' in that moment, told me I wasn't worth anythin' to him no more. He dropped my arms, replacin' them over my throat.

My arms were so much shorter than his I couldn't reach him to push away. My brain throbbed; my veins collapsed. I knew I was turnin' blue. I mouthed his name, beggin' him to stop. Not knowin' he already had.

My body went numb; arms, legs, and feet. I didn't think I could turn my neck either. I was like them dolls they got paradin' up at malls, wearin' their merchandise fer customers to see. I really wasn't far off from them ragdolls. I tried runnin' away, but how stupid was I.

Hunter punched my stomach and I shrimped inward towards the floor to hold myself. He picked up my head with the short hair I had left and I opened my mouth to tell him I wanted to die, but I didn't have time. He slammed the back of my head into the door and my concussed eyes widened.

He was runnin' round me, gatherin' up things I never thought were important. He scrambled up and down the stairs, in and out of the rooms. I stared into the dark livin' room while listenin' to doors slam, furniture break, and his voice cuss words all throughout the echo of my thoughts.

It sounded like I had gone up with him, that it was my body bein' thrown round. My neck started unstiffenin', think that's what got the rest of me to soften up. I grunted as I used my arm to sit my back upright with the door that promised me an unforgivin' future.

"Ya really messed up bad, June" Hunter whispered comin' down the stairs.

He carried a large bag on his back and somethin' large in his free hand. I couldn't see what he was draggin' 'round with him, but the loud scent hit me before he could. It was gas. He was pourin' it all throughout the house after comin' down the stairs with it.

I turned my neck and upper body 'round, scratchin' at the door handle to open it up. My core was weak and I fell face first into the floor with tears pourin' out my eyes. Hunter was in no mood, he looked down at me and threw the large canister towards the couch.

He picked me up by the arm and told me I'd better get to walkin' with him. He opened the front door and cold air split my body into two, knockin' whatever remainin' air I had outta my lungs. I faced the night fields with a sliver of light from the moon to guide me.

A boot hit my back and I tumbled forward onto the hardwood porch, until I rolled my way down the three stairs and onto the gravel. I laid lookin' up at the sky until Hunter picked me up. He curled his fingers 'round mine and I cursed at myself fer enjoyin' the small bundle of heat his palms gave me.

We stopped a few yards from the house and he bent down, causin' me to fall with him. He was breathin' heavy, I ain't even able to hear myself. I watched with screamin' and panicked eyes as he pulled out a lighter from his pocket and lit the ground.

A red and orange like flame quickly danced on the ground towards the house like it was nobody's business. It hit the porch first, spreadin' out over the stairs one by one until it lit the door. Hunter grabbed onto my hand and pulled me up, tellin' me to keep it movin'.

I couldn't.

Cause the one thing I'd been askin' fer, to escape that hell-hole, was finally happenin'. I was dead weight Hunter couldn't get rid of. He dragged my body as I watched the house set ablaze. Wood, glass, everythin' shattered and a burst of divine energy lifted our bodies and slammed us to the ground, apart from each other.

"June!" Hunter yelled fer me.

I was so cold; I couldn't even move. The snow hadn't come yet, but it felt as if it already had. I stared up at the night sky, countin' stars and wishin' they'd lift me to them.

I laid in the small indent my malnourished body created, surrounded by cornstalks I'd never wish to visit again.

He called my name again and again, but it was the small and faint whisper of a child that begged me to keep movin'.

"Don't let my sacrifice go to waste" she whispered into my ear.

Immediately my body started to warm, strength came back to my bones, and I was runnin' on the last bit of adrenaline my soul possessed. I grunted and bit my lip as I flipped over to my hands and knees, crawlin' away as quietly and fast as I could.

I didn't know where I was headin', just as long as Hunter's voice quieted in the distance, I knew I was better off. I didn't care that I was scrappin' up my legs and arms on broken stalks. I didn't care that I was soon to freeze my way towards deaths door than to be found by him.

"I should've left ya in that house" his voice was near.

I stopped in my tracks like a deer sniffin' a human in the air. I thought I was goin' away from him, but turned out I couldn't even leave him correctly. I huddled closer to the ground, tryin' to listen fer his feet snappin' old earth, but he knew the land better than anyone.

My heart beat outta my chest as I waited fer him to pass, make movement, sound, anythin'. It was the longest wait of my life, and he knew I wasn't good at hide and go seek. I was quiet, so quiet, I hadn't realized that maybe he left me.

Maybe he thought I died.

Oh, how naïve and foolish was I.

Two feet snapped on corn stalk corpses off in the distance and I held my breath. I tried lookin' fer them, but got nothin' back. It was too dark, there were too many darn corn stalks, and my eyes were already tired from the night.

"Millie?" a voice whispered and my heart sank deep into my stomach.

I looked 'round and 'round, tryin' to see if it was God playin' tricks on me. I knew it was a trap, so I kept mine closed. I scrunched my eyes and told myself it ain't real. I swore at God and told him it wasn't funny.

I heard another whisper off far away, but it was a mumble, and then another. They were two voices arguin' back and forth about the girl who ran away. One was Hunter, I knew him better than I knew myself. The other was a mystery to me, and fer all I knew, it could've just been him talkin' to himself.

Until the gunshots fired.

I picked up my head and sat on my heels. The frosted soil ate at my skin and told me I'd soon freeze if I didn't move.

I heard 'em knockin' each other down, huffin' and puffin' like some gladiators durin' battle. Their bodies clashed, fists broke, and mouths screamed fer two different names belongin' to me. *I'm right here* I wanted to say but couldn't.

Fer all I knew, I was hallucinatin'. Havin' a nightmare in his room again.

"Millie" he screamed.

Colton screamed.

My eyes snapped wide and my head jerked up. He was here, so close, and I was free to run to him. I used my arms to push myself onto my knees and my weak body said no, but my mind was strong enough to cry yes.

"Colton" I whispered.

Their grunts were comin' closer, all I had to do was wait fer the right moment. But that was just it, there never was a 'right' moment, and there never would be. That's the pain in waitin', it never works out in my favor.

A single gunshot, and then another, a body fell to the ground while the other celebrated egotistically as he's always done. But a body fell to the ground, and it wasn't his, it wasn't that of my capturer.

Just one.

The wrong one.

"Millie" Colton screamed with no air. "Run".

Run, run, run.

I shot up and my head turned in and out of itself. I grabbed onto the sides of my head and bit down a cry that was too good to ruin my chances at ever makin' it out. If Colton was here, that meant others were too. It meant there was more than one lookin' fer me.

A cold hand grabbed onto my ankle and I fell to the frosted ground with a loud scream. I was tryin' to exaggerate all I could, call whoever was with us to my corpse.

He dragged me towards him and my sweater lifted, scrappin' my bare stomach across the hard earth. I let out another scream as he flipped me 'round and grabbed onto my waist. He stared down at me as if he liked it, like he wanted to take his time and savor the moment.

"Yer too good fer yer own good, June" he bit his lip and hurled me up.

I weakly ran with him, practically let him drag my body like dead weight behind him. He kept tellin' me how he wished he would've just kept me in that house. I wondered if I wished fer it too. Maybe I could've gotten out, he would've left, and I could've saved myself.

"Get in the car" he threw my body in front of the door to his old and beat-up truck.

I could hardly lift my weight as he threw some bags into the back, waitin' fer me to hurry it up. He said he wasn't playin' round, that I was causin' too much of a wreak. I stared at the pebbles and dirt I knew was coated across my skin and it wasn't until I heard the click that made me get up.

"I'm not playin' no games" he whispered.

I looked up at him, only seein' the low silhouette of a man pointin' a gun at me. There was a high possibility he was gonna shoot me. I already ruined his life by not submittin', not givin' him a baby, and by callin' the cops.

I was a slug gettin' up, takin' my time, pretendin' to be more injured than I was. My tears weren't fake though, they were streamin' too quick fer me to count. Hunter grabbed me by the weak arm and grounded me on my feet.

He opened the creaky passenger door and told me to get in. I looked at him with a whimperin' lip and his eyes softened fer just a crack in time before regainin' his composure. Still, it was enough to tell me he wasn't gonna kill me.

He punched me in the face, crackin' my nose and warmin' my skin with hot blood. I almost fell, but he caught me, tossin' me into the truck like a bag of dried up potatoes. I quickly looked 'round fer somethin' and God soon answered.

My bare feet were hoverin' over a blanket of broken glass. I looked round fer Hunter, but couldn't find him. Just as I reached fer the handle to leave, his gun fired and then another. He jumped into the car and I watched slow beads of sweat fall down his face.

With both hands on the wheel, he stared off into the distance. The truck wasn't on, nor did he say a word. My fist tightened around the door's handle and the leather under my skin squeaked. My heart stopped, lips parted, and I called myself a dumb girl.

"Get yer hand away from that there handle, June" he cussed.

An anger lit up in my stomach and I grabbed harder onto the handle. He told me to let it go again and again, still I didn't. I also didn't open it either, *coward.* He said his name fer me again and told me I was bein' irrational, that I was the reason to blame fer the house and us needin' to move so quickly.

He told me I was tired, that we'd talk in the mornin'. I was confused why the sudden change, till I looked over and saw he was preparin' some kinda injection to get me with.

It was the stars shinin' on the long and thin silver metal that caught my attention. If it were like the others, I'd have only a few moments until I was out. I needed a distraction, it's all I had.

"That's not my name" I whispered.

In less than a second, my face flew into the glove compartment, rebreakin' my nose and splittin' my lip. He held onto the back of my head, pushin' it further and further, as deeply as he could into that there compartment.

"See what ya made me do, love".

I whimpered a scream, only to cover up the sounds I was makin'. Havin' my head so low gave me to perfect opportunity to grab onto a large piece of glass that was on the floor. I held so firmly onto it that it sliced through my palm and the backs of my fingers.

"My name isn't June!".

I swung the makeshift blade at his face and missed, only to end up pinnin' it straight into his thigh, too far away from his heart to celebrate. Hunter dropped his gun and groaned, lookin' at me with the devil in his eyes.

I pried my hands off the glass and drew in a sharp breath before lookin' at him one last time. With a sting, less than a second was all I needed fer me to know he was gonna kill me now, that there was nothin' I could do or say that'd save me if he ever found me again.

I jumped out the car and stumbled on my toes as I ran down the makeshift driveway, headin' back into fields of corn and tryin' to stay on path. I didn't hear Hunter comin' after me, didn't hear no sounds but my own breathin' and loud feet.

I tripped over a rock and fell face first onto the ground. I let out a cry much louder than I had meant fer it to be, but I couldn't be helped. My foot was mangled when I looked back at the rock that wasn't one of God's beautiful creations. It was one of them coiled spring traps.

It was snagged on my ankle and any movement caused it to dig much deeper. I turned to my side and threw up whatever was left in my stomach before wipin' my mouth with shaky hands. I ain't never used one of them traps, so I didn't know what to do.

I moved my body towards my ankle and bit down on my closed fist to manage some of the pain that couldn't be helped. I was stuck, trapped in a device I should've known how to get outta. Just as I reached once more to release it, a pain surged up the bone in my ankle and through my spine.

I screamed and fell onto my back, legs shakin' and head throbbin'. It was pinchin' harder and harder with each move I made. I thought it was alive, like a hungry coyote tastin' flesh fer the first time.

I laid there in pain, starin' up at the sky, lettin' the cold eat away at my skin. The stars shined brightly over my body and I tried countin' them to distract myself. I tried pushin' myself outta my body and into God's hands, but he wouldn't take me so lightly.

"Millie?" a strange voice called.

A strange yet familiar voice indeed, callin' me home with his warm voice that tasted like sweet honeysuckle. It wasn't God, nor was it the man claimin' to love me with unmatched power, it was Colton.

"Is that you?" his feet moved closer.

I heard him swishin' through the tall stalks, snappin' them down with his feet. He was too loud not to hear, not to smile about. He was comin' to save me, but somethin' deep down told me it wasn't gonna last very long.

"Millie?" he whispered. "Let me know it's you".

If I told him where I was he'd see me at my worst. Given a chance to run and I did, straight into one of Hunter's traps.

And it was all my fault.

Yet pride wasn't anythin' I could find myself carin' about in that moment. Pride was somethin' I didn't care about at all. I was goin' to die if I didn't say anythin', but yet, I wasn't ready to live. I was a complete and useless anomaly to myself.

"Please help me" was all I could say.

He asked where I was, kept tellin' me to make noise. I could only cry, let him hear my silent tears fall down my face as a means to help him. He was gettin' closer though, I could taste it in my bones. A cool breeze rushed up my spine and over my bare legs, I could've sworn that to be true if not fer his scent that embraced me first.

"Millie?" he stood over my body, coverin' the stars from my sight.

I shook my head up and down and cried when he scrambled to his hands and knees. It was as if all my doubts, fears, and pains were bein' carried on his back now. His eyes fell to my trapped ankle and he swore under his breath.

"You're gonna take a deep breath in, wait fer me to count to three, then let go of that air, okay?" he whispered by my feet.

I shook my head and clenched my teeth so I could whisper I understood without havin' to make much noise. He placed his hands on the animal trap and my eyes shot open.

"I know it hurts, Millie" he stroked my other leg. "It's going to hurt before it gets better".

Gunshots fired off into the distance and I knew he was comin' fer me, I knew he was lookin' fer me to kill himself. Colton told me it could be his men, that they were all here fer me.

I nodded and laid back down fer him to do whatever he needed, and I took a deep breath in. His breath swayed and I knew his hands were shakin'. He counted to three and I released everythin' I knew was stored up and the trap screeched open.

It tore at my skin and the scabbed pieces that already wrapped round it. I sat up screamin' and pulled my legs to my chest, hand shakin' and all as I tried feelin' around the wound. It was mangled, needed stiches, and I was gonna be surprised if I could still keep it by the end of everythin'.

"We're going to get you out of here" Colton took off his coat and draped it across my legs.

I let out a soft moan as the warmth from his coat soothed my frozen legs and he positioned his body so I could lean on his stomach. He raised an arm, rockin' my body closer to him and he spoke into a small black box attached to his chest.

"Suspect armed and running".

"And Millie?" a woman spoke a few seconds later.

"With me" he responded. "No eyes on the suspect".

Their voices ceased and he held me tighter, apologizin' fer the years he wasn't there. I couldn't even say nothin' to him. He was blamin' himself fer somethin' I did. He was blamin' himself fer somethin' that was my fault. He even tried tellin' me it wasn't my burden to carry.

"You're safe now, Millie" he kissed the back of my hand.

"Say it again" I whispered more to myself than him.

"You're safe".

"No" my eyes met his. "Say my name".

"Millie" he leaned in near.

Guns fired more rapidly, closer to us and I jumped each time, further from Colton's hard grasp. I thought I would've been used to it by now, but it seemed I wasn't. Their voices yelled closer too, Hunter's was much nearer than I thought he would've been. Then again, he always found me.

I think I even heard bodies droppin' like flies on the wall, but it was just my heart. It could feel him, told me when the danger was comin'. I shifted in Colton's arms and he told me it was gonna be okay.

"No" I whispered. "We have to get outta here".

"My men are on it" he whispered back, usin' his thumb to wipe away my silent tears. "You're safe now".

My heart increased, my breathin' failed, and I tried pushin' him off me. He sighed and looked at the ground, tellin' me we could leave if I really wanted to. I nodded against him and he helped me stand. The coat dropped to my feet and Colton picked it up, puttin' 'round my shoulders.

"Let's go-" he managed to say before the gun rang through my head.

His body hit mine, knockin' me to the ground and I screamed. His eyes blinked and his mouth opened wide, breathin' like I had been all night. I grabbed onto his face and told him to stay with me. He tried tellin' me to run.

"Yer never gonna leave me, June" Hunter cocked the gun back once more. "What'd ya think ya could have yer happy endin' without me?".

He raised the barrel at Colton's head and I jumped in front of him.

"Please" I cried. "I'll go with you, just let him be".

"I'm not takin' ya with me, June" he motioned with the gun fer me to move. "I just wanna see ya suffer one last time".

"I won't move" I was too brave fer my own good.

"Fair enough".

His gun stared me in the eyes and I said goodbye quickly to the girl I could've been before everythin' happened. Most importantly, I said goodbye to the girl I was. The one who was brave enough to get me outta that house.

Just as the gun fired, Colton rolled from underneath me and over. My eyes pierced into his and he smiled with a fool's laugh before closin' his eyes and restin' his head on my lap. I let out a loud skriek and looked back at Hunter.

His body was on the ground, blood comin' up from his mouth. Colton told me it was gonna be okay and I was more confused than ever. A woman ran from the stalks towards us, askin' if we were okay. I told her Colton was shot, that he was dyin'.

"I'm okay" he sat up. "Just nicked me in the shoulder, that's all. Thank you, Becca".

The woman stood firm and gave us a smile before talkin' into her radio, sayin' that we'd need an ambulance. I crawled outta Colton's arms and to Hunter. He lifted a hand and only God knows why I took it.

A smile beaded his lips and warm and red blood poured too fast outta it. He was dyin', I smiled wider than I ever had. He began coughin', turnin' on his back and reachin' towards me. I let him touch my face, let him wipe his bloodied hands over my skin because I knew it was the last time he was ever gonna.

His hand fell limp and his body rocked back. I swear I saw his soul bein' ripped from his skin and dragged to hell where it belonged. I swear one of the Devil's demons winked at me before drinkin' his soul and laughin' his way to Hades.

Everythin' that happened from there was fast. The red and blue lights from the ambulance lit up the entire field. My body went limp and the last thing I remembered was Colton carryin' me towards the stretcher. I raised my hand to caress his soft skin, but he held it in his hand and kissed my palm.

I opened my eyes I didn't know had closed and just before them ambulance doors closed, I got the chance to see it. The field of corn I was trapped and imprisoned in, set in flames. Hell had to take everythin' from him, includin' my prison.

My eyes closed fer the very last time and I smiled.

And I cried.

Because he didn't even get to suffer, he took the easy way out by dyin' that night.

I could only hope that hell was goin' to be hotter.

EPILOGUE

"You're safe now" she took my hand. "Please wake up, Millie Maye. Mama's outside right now and she wants to see ya. I wanna see ya".

I couldn't open my eyes, nor could I move, reach fer her, tell her that I was here. I was asleep, wanderin' through a world covered by white light. I didn't need to sleep, eat, or drink. I was simply existin'.

And so I closed my eyes in the dream and I let God's angels carry me off to another world I was soon to rejoin. I wandered around until a little girl joined me. She ran into my arms and I pecked a kiss onto her forehead. We listened to Abilene together, sat on the floor or floated above it while we smiled at her words.

"I promise I won't make ya dress up with me" she cried. "I'll even go the day without wearin' any makeup, ya said ya like me with my bare face. How about ya wake up and tell me again? I just wanna see ya smile, sis".

The little girl and I laughed together at Abilene's crazy stories, even cried together too when she told us she was gettin' married but refused to have the weddin' until I was there beside her through it all. She squeezed my hand and we tried squeezin' her back, but our souls didn't have bodies to touch.

She told us that Colton drugged Hunter that night. Got him drunk and followed him back to the house. Said he never gave up, even when she thought she was gonna, he kept her and mama goin'.

Abilene fell quiet, and so did my visitor. The little girl told me she had to go and I stood up, askin' her to wait. She smiled, and without movin' her lips, told me I didn't need her right now.

"Right now?" I whispered. "What do you mean?".

"I'll be back, mama".

I reached fer her, but my hand fell through her soul and she floated away like lilac petals in the wind. Her laugh echoed in my body, restin' in my heart, promisin' this wasn't the end fer us.

She was my reason for stayin' alive.

She was the reason I survived fer as long as I did.

"Won't you open your eyes fer me?" her voice started my heart once more and blood pumped through every inch of my bein'.

I'm comin' fer you, please don't leave yet. Nauseatin' waves twitched my skin and my arms and legs too. I heard her gasp, heard them all cry in the room 'round me. Every pain I left behind was now comin' back to me and I groaned fer them.

Her hand on mine, another by my feet, and one more at my other side. I felt them all so vividly, felt them all as if they were individually attached to me. My lungs forced themselves to take a sharp and painful breath because they knew my journey from here on out wasn't gonna be an easy one.

I knew Hunter was always gonna be with me. Even if he was dead, he'd still find ways to break into my subconscious and peel away at my sanity. It wasn't gonna be easy, gettin' rid of him. But maybe I didn't have to, maybe I had to accept him, adapt to what he'd done, and act as if I was the one who came out alive.

Because I was.

I had stolen time to make up fer; years of love with Abe and mama, and a forever with Colton I was just gettin' started with. They were home, and I was supposed to be gettin' back.

My eyes shot open and hers were the first I saw. Covered in tears, lips whimperin', and old crow's feet smilin'.

"Millie!" mama screamed. "You're home, my sweet baby girl. It's all gonna be okay now".

I didn't know if I was ever gonna be okay after what I endured, but if the creek don't rise, I sure as heck knew one thing.

I'm home.

ABOUT THE AUTHOR

Olesia Parker is a self-taught writer that has 'dipped her toes' in almost everything. After completing and publishing her first trilogy, The Damned, Olesia has taken off to starting many more writings. Thus, the Corn Maze being her first novel published as a single work.

TO YOU, THE READER

Thank you for enduring the pains of Millie Maye and reading her story. May you know that you are never alone on your journey.

Ever.

OTHER WORKS
OLESIA PARKER

The Damned Trilogy
- ❖ Escaping Death
- ❖ Remember Their Voices, Remember Their Faces
- ❖ Haven

Corn Maze

Made in the USA
Las Vegas, NV
02 January 2023